*From Deneen
for my birthday*

IN SEARCH OF YESTERDAY

JOYCE MACBETH MOREHOUSE

In Search Of Yesterday

by Joyce Macbeth Morehouse

©1987 Word Aflame Press
Hazelwood, MO 63042-2299

Cover Design by Tim Agnew
Illustrated by Michael Caito

All Scripture quotations in this book are from the King James Version of the Bible unless otherwise identified.

All rights reserved. No portion of this publication may be reproduced, stored in an electronic system, or transmitted in any form or by any means, electronic, mechanical, photocopy, recording, or otherwise, without the prior permission of Word Aflame Press. Brief quotations may be used in literary reviews.

Printed in United States of America.

Printed by

Library of Congress Cataloging-in-Publication Data

Morehouse, Joyce.
   In search of yesterday.

   I. Title.
PR9199.3.M637I5 1987   823'.914   87-14741
ISBN 0-932581-17-X

Dedication

To Mom and Dad whose love and creativity instilled in me my love for literature.

Contents

1. Ashes to Ashes–*7*
2. Unexpected Discovery–*11*
3. Diary Disclosures–*17*
4. Search Begins–*21*
5. Discouraging News–*25*
6. Plans for a Journey–*29*
7. Flight West–*37*
8. Encounter with Miss Claire–*43*
9. A Visit to Neuberg Town Hall–*49*
10. In Search of Betty Schmitt–*53*
11. Another Boarding House–*59*
12. Introduction to Church–*65*
13. Pleasant Surroundings–*69*
14. An Unpleasant Topic–*73*
15. Chilled to the Bone–*77*
16. Two Weeks Till Christmas–*81*
17. Disappointing Discovery–*87*
18. Confronting Miss Claire–*91*
19. A Step in the Right Direction–*99*
20. Chilling News–*103*
21. Life and Death Situation–*107*
22. Back at Miss Claire's–*111*
23. Alternate Arrangements–*115*
24. Filling the Gap–*121*
25. Home at Last–*127*
26. Kin-Folks–*131*

CHAPTER 1

Ashes to Ashes

*L*oren Neilsen buttoned the top button of her new gray coat against the penetrating November chill. She shivered involuntarily and held a soggy handkerchief to her tear-blurred eyes. She tried to grasp the reality of it all as the minister droned, "Ashes to ashes and dust to dust," but it was still an ugly nightmare. Surely she would awaken from the unreality of it all tomorrow.

Tomorrow—without Dad! She burst into a torrent of fresh tears, and then friends were surrounding her, voicing muffled phrases of comfort. Someone gently took her arm and led her toward a waiting vehicle. As much as she wanted to do so, she could not bring herself to look back, but sat with head bowed, crying softly, as the automobile began its slow return to the land of the living. Her imagination rang with the dull thuds of the scoops of earth striking the casket's surface, and the odor of floral tributes filled her nostrils. She tried to turn off her thoughts. It was over. There was no way she could bring him back, and cruel as it seemed, life would still go on for her. She would just have to pick up the pieces.

Her friend Cathy watched the pale, drawn face. It was full of weariness and despair. The cornflower blue eyes were red-rimmed and swollen. Even her normally springy auburn curls drooped lifelessly on her shoulders, and her slender five-foot frame had a pathethic stoop.

"John and I will come in for a while, Loren," her friend broke the silence, "or perhaps you'd rather spend the night with us."

Loren shook her head. "No, I've got to face...being alone sometime. It might as well be now. No sense in putting it off."

"There's a whole evening ahead of you. You need someone there, so we'll still come in for a while."

Tears glistened in Loren's eyes. "I've got to face it sometime, Cathy, but...if you like..."

The young couple followed her inside. Someone, perhaps her next-door neighbor, had already been there and left a plate of sandwiches and sweets for a snack. Upon seeing them Loren realized she had not eaten for the past two days, and now she felt a pang of hunger.

Cathy scurried about and soon had the kettle boiling and the table set for the three of them. She kept hoping someone else would drop in to ease the strained silence, but knew it was highly unlikely, for Loren had very few close friends. She had recently broken off her long-term engagement with her boyfriend, and he had already married someone else on the rebound. She was just beginning to get over the trauma of that experience when her dad took suddenly ill. In a matter of days the perforated ulcer had filled his system with poison, and by the time Loren came home one night to find him unconscious on the floor, it was too late to do anything for him. She couldn't believe it when the doctor came out of the emergency room and told her the facts.

Cathy knew that Loren was blaming herself for not persuading him to see a doctor sooner. While she prepared the lunch, she kept a wary eye on her friend, who sat curled up in the armchair, a look of total dejection on her face. John was making a great pretense of reading the newspaper.

"Come and get it!" Cathy called.

Loren made a feeble effort to rise, her languor so obvious that Cathy fought an effort to get up and assist her.

"Loren, I wish you wouldn't stay here alone tonight. You really should have someone with you. What about Hazel?"

"I'd rather not, Cathy. If you don't mind, I need to be alone."

"But you've been alone for the past few days! There's no need to torture yourself, you know. You do have friends who care about you. You're perfectly welcome to stay with us."

"I know, and I appreciate friends like you two, but I need to get used to this."

"Don't make her feel pressured, Cathy—though she's welcome to stay with us." John added the afterthought quickly lest Loren misinterpret what he had said.

Loren looked at John, her eyes brimming with unshed tears. "Thanks, John. Thanks to both of you for being here when I needed someone. But. . .I have to come to grips with this. . . It might as well be now." She went back to her sandwich with difficulty, and they finished eating in silence.

Afterward, while they cleaned up, Cathy could restrain herself no longer. "I know it's soon to ask, Loren, but why don't you just move in with us. You really haven't any close friends, except Hazel, and she's so far out of town."

"Please, Cathy. I'd rather not talk about it. I'm so tired tonight, I can't even think—and actually I don't want to think!"

"I'm sorry, Loren. I had no business bringing it up. Why don't you go straight to bed and see if you can't get a decent night's rest? I think John and I will stop off a minute at his mother's, then go home and go straight to bed ourselves. It will be great to go to bed early for a change."

The door had barely closed on her retreating friends when Loren threw herself, fully clothed, across the bed. A great sense of loneliness brought a fresh surge of tears, but her weariness overcame that, and with a final great effort she reached down and pulled the covers over her.

CHAPTER

2

Unexpected Discovery

Morning sunlight was streaming through the bedroom window, the world was a peaceful place. Then it hit her! She was alone—absolutely alone! No coffee aroma came from the kitchen, no soft radio music, no off-key whistling. Anger rose up in her. Why was the morning bright and clear? The sun had no right to shine today! Everything she loved was gone! Life was empty! Not a single relative remained, to her knowledge. At one point, her father had mentioned something about a grandmother, but she'd likely be dead by now. Anyway, she could never trace her; she didn't even know her name.

How long ago had it been? She must have been thirteen or fourteen. She searched her memory. It was that period of her life when she had been so difficult. Her dad had threatened to send her west to live with her German grandmother.

"If she wasn't such a religious fanatic," he'd said, "for

two cents I'd send you to get a taste of her discipline."

Painfully, Loren recalled the scene. She knew she had been difficult and unreasonable, but life seemed to be using her so unfairly. Her mother had died only the year before, and she and her father had quarrelled constantly, it seemed, about her lack of responsibility and everything else that accompanied those early adolescent years. In addition, her father's only reference to her mother's family had been to his mother-in-law, and Loren got the impression he hated her. She had finally dared ask why he felt this way, and his answer had left her as puzzled as ever.

"I'd rather not talk about it. She didn't want another baby. Just be thankful I was willing to give you a name!" For a while she seethed with rage, angry mostly at what his statement implied but irritated as well by his lack of communication on the subject. Why couldn't he tell her about her mother's family? As she thought about it, she realized that she had never heard her mother discuss her family either—not even the German grandmother. Gradually, the loss of her mother dulled, and she was able to put it out of her mind. Her ability to get along with her father developed with her maturity, and life began to get back to normal. Now, with her father gone, she wished their harmonious relationship had blossomed sooner.

With a good deal of effort, Loren pushed her feet over the side of the bed and felt around for her slippers. They were out of reach, so she finally had to sit up and slip them on. She felt horrible and wished she could spend the day in bed, but that would solve nothing. She dreaded the day ahead and spent as much time in her bath as she possibly could. When the water was finally too cold for comfort,

Unexpected Discovery

she forced herself to begin the day's tasks.

Though the thought of food seemed repulsive to her, the percolating coffee managed to awaken her taste buds, and she popped a slice of bread into the toaster. Over toast and coffee she laid out plans for the necessary things in her future. When she could find the courage, she had to call the landlord and find out when the rental lease expired. That would raise another problem. If it was in three months, as she believed it to be, then she had to give notice that she wished to move at the end of November. She felt she could not stay there any longer. She wanted to move closer to the office. It suddenly occurred to her that perhaps her father had a copy of the lease somewhere in his files.

Loren gathered up the dishes and slipped them into the sink, then made her way into the solitary office. One glance at the empty office chair brought tears to her eyes, but she forced herself to maintain control and picked up her father's big key ring, trying each key in the safe while valiantly fighting her feelings. The lock clicked, and she pulled out the bottom drawer to begin her search. She felt something akin to a sense of guilt. This was something she had never done before. In addition, it appeared to be futile. The old folders turned up nothing that even looked like a lease.

The last file folder contained numerous papers that were old and yellowed. She quickly pushed them back into place without examining anything, but in the process her hand touched a hard surface. She pulled the drawer forward and took a look at the thing she had touched. It was a box. She withdrew it carefully and to her dismay found an old family Bible inside. Although it looked old, it obviously was almost untouched. She flipped back the rigid cover and saw an inscription that sent her mind soaring: "On the occasion of your sixteenth birthday. To Elsie from Mom, with love. (Read it every day and let it guide you.)"

This was her mother's Bible—and she had never known about it! Slowly, almost reverently, she turned the pages. There was a section on births and deaths and even a space for marriages. Under the latter was recorded her own parents' marriage, and under the death category was the notation, "Hans Iven Schmitt, August 2, 1926." That had to be her grandfather! Even though her father had spoken of her German grandmother, it had not occurred to Loren that her grandfather had also been German.

She read on in the birth section. The words "Baby Schmitt" had been written and then a line placed through them. Underneath was "Loren Elizabeth Neilsen, September 3, 1950." Was that the original entry for her birth?

Curious, she sought for further information. Her efforts produced an old marriage certificate with a second ragged paper stapled to it. Her heart tattooing madly, Loren checked the information.

"Bride: Elsie Noreen Schmitt, born in Neuberg, April 9, 1934.

"Groom: Henry Dean Neilsen, born in Frankton, February 1, 1930." On the attached paper was information regarding the parents of both bride and groom. Her father's parents, Loren learned, had been born in Frankton, New Brunswick, and were recorded as Helen Irene Neilsen (Freed) and Benjamin Ellis Neilsen. Her maternal grandparents were registered as Elizabett Ann Schmitt (Herman) and Hans Iven Schmitt, each born in

Unexpected Discovery

Neuberg, Manitoba.

The phone rang, and Loren jumped nervously. It was Cathy wondering how she had spent the night. "Hi, Loren. You OK?"

"Fine, Cathy, and you?"

"Well, I spent a great deal of time worrying about how you were resting."

"Oh, I did fine. Actually, I was afraid I might not be able to get to sleep, but I went out like a light. I was exhausted."

"I'm glad to hear that. How're you doing today?"

"I...I think I've found some leads on some relatives, Cathy!"

"Hey! You're kidding! How did you manage that?"

"Well, in looking for the rent lease I came across my parents' marriage certificate and some other information. It says Dad's relatives are from Frankton, New Brunswick. That's not so far away!... Oh no...I remember now! I vaguely recall his telling me that his parents moved back to Sweden when I was just little. I don't think they communicated much, but somehow, I think they died there. Oh, why did I have to remember that now? Just when I thought I was onto something!"

"That's too bad, Loren. But what about your Mom's folks?"

"I'm...not sure. It's possible I have a grandmother. I've heard her mentioned, but she's out west somewhere."

"Maybe there's something you can do to contact her."

"I doubt it. Say, Cathy, why don't you run over here, and we'll go through this stuff. I sort of hate doing it by myself."

"OK! See you in a jiffy!"

Sudden remorse filled Loren as she hung up the receiver. Now why did she invite someone else to go through these personal things. It was bad enough for her to do it!

CHAPTER

3

Diary Disclosures

The two friends spent the rest of the forenoon going through the files, but they yielded no further information. Loren found further reason to regret her impulsive decision to invite Cathy to help in the search, for she knew that Cathy would realize the date on her parents' marriage certificate was seven months prior to her birth. It was something Cathy didn't need to know, but Loren quickly pushed it out of her mind. There were more important things to feel remorseful about.

"Loren, if I were you, I know what I'd do."

"Yeah?"

"I'd take a lead from this certificate and try to locate your Grandmother Schmitt. After all, it's only in western Canada. It's not like you'd have to go to some foreign country to find her."

"I suppose you're right, but I'm not sure how I should go about it. Things like that aren't done every day."

"There've got to be people who trace missing relatives. Why don't you write to that place, Neuberg Town Hall, or what-have-you, and ask if they have any records on E. Schmitt? They'll get back to you one way or another. At least you'll know if she's dead or alive."

Loren nodded. "I think I'll just forget it for today. I couldn't go for a while anyway. I've already had a week off work."

They started putting things back in the files.

"Wait!" Cathy ordered. "Let's do this a bit more carefully or we'll not get these drawers closed again. There's a lot of stuff here!"

As it was, the lower drawer would not close, so they emptied it out and started over. At last, they pushed the neatly stacked file drawer. It refused to budge.

"Hey! Hold it! I see the problem." Cathy was down on her hands and knees prying at something. A small red book finally came loose in her hand.

Loren's eyes filled with tears. "A diary! I can't believe it! And it's initialled E. N. S. It must be Mother's."

Cathy pushed the drawer closed and got up. "I'll leave you to look it over in privacy. It's lunchtime and I have to run. John'll be home and no lunch ready."

"Oh, I'm sorry, Cathy. That was inconsiderate of me. I should have thought. . ."

Cathy held up a restraining hand. "No problem. I'll just fix a sandwich. Say, why don't you come over this evening?"

"Well. . .I don't know."

"It'll do us all good! See you later." Cathy left hurriedly in an attempt to beat the clock and her husband's arrival for lunch.

Diary Disclosures

Loren took the diary in both hands, reluctant to open it, yet curious to know just what it contained that might help her locate a relative. Maybe it would answer many of the questions she had wanted to ask all her life. What would Dad say if he could know she had found this? He had never offered to let her read it, even in later years. What did it conceal?

Loren felt almost as if she were betraying her father's trust. A great sadness enveloped her as she moved about the kitchen in a mechanical effort to prepare something for her own lunch. She filled the kettle with water and got out her coffee mug, diary still in hand. Maybe she could bring herself to read it over a good, stiff cup of coffee—the blacker, the better. Without thinking she reached for her father's mug as well, then fought back tears as she remembered he wouldn't be home for lunch—ever.

Loren opened the diary to the flyleaf and read the inscription: "Elsie N. Schmitt, Christmas 1948. Five-Year Diary." On the inside cover were a number of hearts with the initals E. S. and no two others alike. Loren realized that she hadn't known her mother very well, although she had been twelve years old when her mother passed away. Reading the first few entries made her feel guilty and heartsick. Her mother had been a mere teen-ager at the time, but she was not hesitant about expressing her inmost desires. The first day's entry was New Year's Day, 1949: "Ma threatened to kill me if I went to the New Year's ball with Don, but I went anyway. . .really whooped it up! Have a head bigger than a pumpkin this morning, so I paid for my fun. Mom can't stand Don, but she only said she was disappointed and was 'praying' for me. Her usual line."

Loren skipped through the pages, scanning each year's first entry as she went. It appeared that the beginning of every year was spent the same way with wild partying and a mother-daughter conflict, but then according to other entries, Loren learned that the mother-daughter conflict was a common occurrence. From what she read, she couldn't help but understand that her mother had been a wild, rebellious teen-ager—so unlike the loving mother she had known. Perhaps she had learned a lesson along the way, or she certainly had changed.

Feeling as though she was losing respect for the mother she remembered, she determined to put the diary away without reading further, but as she was about to close the book an entry caught her eye.

"Nov. 8. Met the sweetest guy at the dance tonight, Henry Dean Neilsen, blond and gorgeous. Asked me for a date Friday night. I tried not to look overanxious, but don't think it worked. I think he knows I flipped. I can hardly wait for Friday."

So. . .that would have been when Mom and Dad met, Loren thought. She put the book away, not wanting to read more. Of one thing she was sure. There were undertones of a constant battle between a mother and a headstrong, self-centered daughter. Loren thought back to her own childhood with her mother, who had been a truly devoted mother. There was never any mention of her earlier life or any reference to her family. She had rarely mentioned her own mother.

Loren wished now that she had never found the incriminating evidence. She certainly regretted having read any of it, and she was afraid of what else it might contain.

CHAPTER

4

Search Begins

*T*he evening with John and Cathy proved anything but a success. They made every effort to draw Loren into their conversation, but she was too preoccupied with other thoughts. She was letting her mind become obsessed with a sense of guilt over having read the diary, which had never been intended for her eyes.

"You know, Cathy, I should never have read any of that diary!"

"Come now, Loren. There couldn't have been anything there that devastating!"

Loren shook her head in a negative motion. "No. Not devastating. Just upsetting."

"Well, if you'll be realistic about things, you must realize that if your mother hadn't intended those things ever to become known she would most likely have destroyed the diary. She did have time for such a thing before she died, didn't she?"

"Uh. . .yes, I guess you're right. That still doesn't change anything. I shouldn't have read it!"

"I'm sure there's nothing there so bad that you can't cope with it. It's just your frame of mind at this time. Along with everything else. . .your dad's passing and all. . .you're just not ready to cope. I suggest you just put it away for a while, then after you've had time to pull things together and are feeling more like it, you can always go back and take a more rational look. It might tell you a whole lot about your family, you know."

"That's what I'm afraid of. Maybe I'd be a lot better off not knowing."

"That's just because of your state of depression, my dear. I'm sure you'd feel a whole lot better if you could only know you had a living relative somewhere—someone you belong to and could turn to right now."

"Yeah, but what if there's no one?"

"Then by the time you find out you may be more capable of dealing with it. I know you're finding these things hard to deal with right now, Loren, but how would you feel if. . .well, maybe I could drop a line to that town office in Manitoba for you. Would that be better?"

Loren perked up at once. "Oh, Cathy, could you. . .I mean, you wouldn't mind?"

"Of course not, if it'll make it any easier for you. What was the name of that place?"

"It's Neuberg, Manitoba, and my grandmother's name is Elizabett Schmitt. Here, I'll write it down for you. I don't know the street address, but I gather it's not a real large place; you know the type. Saturday night dances and holiday affairs seem to be the big thing, so I guess. . .Oh, Cathy, I'm not really sure we should try!"

Search Begins

Cathy smiled. "There's no harm in trying. We should. Definitely. And I will."

Loren's mood picked up a bit, but when she begged weariness and refused to spend the night with them, they took her home. They decided to walk the block in the cool night air, but Loren's hesitancy about letting her friend write on her behalf kept her in a preoccupied state of mind. She went to bed with a headache.

Cathy lost no time in getting a letter ready. If there was anything Loren needed, it was a family member to share her grief, for she had been so close to and so dependent on her father. Cathy sent her first letter to Neuberg Town Hall, in care of the manager, requesting all possible information on a Mrs. Elizabett Schmitt from the area. As best she could, she described the circumstances and gave her return address. She then proceeded to write directly to Mrs. Schmitt, explaining that she was trying to locate any member of her friend's family. Only after she got in bed, her letter already deposited in the post office night box, did she remember that she had forgotten to put Loren's name in the letter. Oh well, she thought, my name and address are included. As long as I get a reply, that is the main thing. If the letter was undeliverable, she hoped it would be returned right away for the waiting would be the worst part for Loren. She had a vague idea it might take months to locate an individual. She hoped nobody would get too impatient with the process.

She was not aware of her restlessness until John uttered a long, weary sigh. "For goodness sake, Cathy, will you stop jumping around so? I've got to get up and go to work in the morning, and you've been running around half the night, writing and posting letters. And you're still jumping around like a jumping jack. Can't you settle down?"

"I'm sorry, John. I've been so busy thinking about Loren and her problems, I didn't realize I was being such a nuisance. I guess I just forgot what time it was. It is rather late, and I am having trouble getting to sleep. I just can't seem to settle down."

His only response was a disgruntled "I'll say!" so she finally got up, pulled a thick comforter from the closet shelf and went out to toss on the couch awhile. At least her restlessness there would not disturb her husband.

The disturbing questions continued to fill her mind. Would she get an answer? If so, would the news be good or bad? Would she inadvertantly uncover discouraging or even devastating information from Loren's past?

The shades of night were beginning to fade when she finally fell asleep.

CHAPTER

5

Discouraging News

Loren's impatience did nothing to hasten a reply to Cathy's letter. During the week following the funeral she navigated between her house and Cathy's as though sleepwalking. Time dragged mercilessly, and try as she might, she could not bring herself to open the diary again. The only real accomplishment, she felt, was to call Mrs. Holmes and give notice of leaving at the end of November. Cathy had come over a few times to help her pack a few items, but even then it was a slow task due to her inability to concentrate on anything as she should.

Although she expressed the desire to put her father's clothes away, the whole process took much longer than it should, for every now and then she would link an item with some past activity and burst into tears. Cathy finally eased the strain by energetically taking charge of the project and helping her finish it. Once her father's belongings were out of sight, Loren found it easier to contend with his not being there.

Loren spent most of the weekend at her friend Hazel's but Monday was still a long time in coming. However, once back at work, things took on a more normal perspective, and she began to look forward to the end of the month when she would no longer have to come back to the familiar surroundings each night.

The last Thursday in November Cathy called the office, but as luck would have it, Loren was out on a break. Cathy left a message to have her stop on the way home.

The rest of the day dragged for Loren. It must be a letter! she thought excitedly. Why else would Cathy call her at work? Loren could scarcely wait. Would her grandmother want her to come? she wondered. Her imagination began playing tricks with her mind until she finally decided, ten minutes before quitting time, that as she was accomplishing nothing she might as well leave.

She didn't wait for Cathy to answer her knock, but burst in with an exuberance she hadn't felt in ages. One look at Cathy caused all her enthusiasm to drain through the soles of her feet.

Cathy waved an envelope. It was addressed to Mrs. Elizabett Schmitt and stamped, "Return to sender. Addressee unknown."

"Sorry, Loren. No luck!"

"Is. . .is that all?"

"All so far. I've never had an answer from the one I sent to Newberg Town Hall. But let me tell you what happened. I went to the library today and did some research. Seems like it's still just a small town, but they did say that most early settlers were German—hence the name Neuberg. They also said that the Germans have mixed and mingled with the inhabitants of the surrounding towns and villages until scarcely a German name remains."

"Oh, doesn't sound too promising, does it? Goodness knows where Grandmother's gone, if she's still alive."

"Well, it's pretty hard to tell what might have become of her. She might even have married again. It seems your grandfather died at a fairly early age, and you said your mother was only sixteen when she left home, so who knows?"

"I suppose you're right, but I wanted so much to find a relative."

Loren sounded so dejected that Cathy insisted she stay and have supper with them. "You're not going to that empty house feeling as you do just now. I'm having pork chops for supper, so I'll just add an extra helping. How was your day at work anyhow?"

"Long. I thought it would never end, though most days go by so slowly. I must admit they are beginning to get back to normal, though. At least I'm starting to keep my mind on what I'm doing most of the time, but nights...they're a different story."

Cathy nodded sympathetically. "That's why I wish you were out of that house. By the way, John said he could come over at noon and help you get moved."

"Oh, really, Cathy? That would be great, although it hardly seems fair that John would have to use his afternoon to move me after he works all Saturday morning. Are you sure it won't be too inconvenient?"

"Not at all! When you first asked and I told you he had to work, I was not aware that it would be for only three hours in the morning. Sometimes he works all day, and there have been times when they've called him to come in after supper, so things worked out just fine for this Saturday. He'll come home for lunch, and then we'll be right over to give you a hand."

"Well, that's certainly a load off my mind. I've tried all week to find someone to help me move, but it seems like everyone wants their Saturday for themselves. I'll never be able to thank you and John enough for your help!"

Cathy patted her friend's arm affectionately. "Let me remind you—that's what friends are for. Don't worry about it! And don't give up on your grandmother yet— who knows what might result from my letter to Neuberg Town Hall!"

CHAPTER 6

Plans for a Journey

Saturday noon, John's car pulled into Loren's, and Cathy ran into the house waving a letter. "It came. My reply from the town hall."

Suddenly Loren's knees felt weak. "What's it say?"

"Well, the manager was very nice. Said they have no Elizabett Schmitt presently in their directory, but he went on to say that there were a number of Schmitts who settled there at the turn of the century. His suggestion is that 'the concerned party drop into my office, and we will do our best to research the files and turn up any pertinent information.' Sounds like he thinks you're right next door instead of two thousand miles away."

"Oh, no." Loren's face was full of disappointment.

"You know, Loren, I hadn't really thought about it, but maybe he's right. Why don't you take some time off and go west for a visit? It'll be good for you from every angle. You do need a rest."

In Search Of Yesterday

"You can't mean it!"

"Well, why not? There's not a thing to stop you."

"Oh, Cathy. . .I can't imagine. . .I'll have to think about it. Besides I just can't get time off whenever I like, and it's so far!"

"I'll tell you what. If I was in your present position and thought I might find a long-lost relative, I'd be willing to forget my job if I had to!"

"Why! I couldn't do that! There I'd be, in a strange town without work!"

"Maybe you could find something there."

Loren shook her head. "This is all too sudden! I've got to have time to think this thing through."

"Well, it seems to be the logical thing to do as far as I can see. Better to go for the information than send for it."

Loren spent a restless night considering the suggestion. At first it seemed so out-of-the-question that she felt certain she could never do it, but the more she thought of the manager's offer of help, the more excited she became at the prospect of tracking down a relative. When she finally decided to ask for a leave of absence from her job, anticipation mounted within her. She dozed off to dream of finding her Grandmother Schmitt only to awaken, with a keen sense of disappointment, to the realization that it was merely a dream.

Loren decided she would not mention her plans to Cathy until all arrangements were final. Maybe she wouldn't be able to get time off anyway. If she did, Hazel would be the first to know, for she was in the same office. Even so, she and Hazel were no longer as close as they had once been. As teen-agers, they had been in-

Plans for a Journey

separable, and it was Hazel who had introduced her to Jim.

Jim—she preferred to forget him, leave him far behind, but life had its sneaky way of bringing things to the remembrance. A deep ache filled the cavity of her chest as she recalled the first time she had brought him home to meet her father. They had really hit it off together. Dad had often invited Jim over after that. That was one reason her father found it so hard to accept when she had broken up with Jim. "Just for a trial time," she had explained. The next thing she knew, Jim was going to be married to the new girl on their street. That's when her father had leased this house, and they had tried to escape the reminders of the past.

Loren shuddered and pulled the covers up under her chin. She spent the rest of the night in a turbulent struggle to go back to sleep, but as the first streaks of dawn lightened the sky, she gave up her fight and forced herself out of bed. Despite all the old memories her mind conjured up, she made herself concentrate on her plans. Now that she had really decided to do something definite about her search for a family member, her plans proceeded a mile a minute. She dared not think what would happen if she were refused her request at work.

The morning was clear and crisp, and she wondered what the weather would be like this time of year in Manitoba. She got out her calendar and began to plan specifically. How she wished her father were here to give her guidance.

Loren resolved to see her boss, Mr. Adson, as soon as she got to work, but all her resolve drained quickly away as she finally approached his office.

"I've come. . .to ask. . .uh. . .for a leave of absence," she managed to stammer.

"Of course! I should have suggested you take some time off. The last while has been hard on you, I'm sure. You've grown pale and listless since...your father's death. I believe the very best remedy we could find would be a break in ritual. You need a rest, Loren."

She was on the verge of tears and could only nod in response. She hadn't expected him to be so fatherly.

"How much time would you like?" He pushed the desk calendar toward her.

"I thought perhaps. . .well, if I could take off starting next Monday. . .and maybe have until the new year?"

"Certainly! No reason why not. One good thing about this time of the year is that our company requires less personnel at this particular season than any other. Insurance sales slump around Christmas, and we can easily get by without you, though you can be sure we'll miss having you around. I do think it's the best possible time for you to take a leave of absence, however."

"Thank you, Mr. Adson. I appreciate that."

"That's quite all right. Sorry I hadn't been the one to think of it sooner. Guess I was just slow to notice, or I would have suggested you should stay home longer after. . .everything happened."

She could have told him her desire was to get back on the job and occupy her mind, but she said nothing.

At the door, he stopped her briefly. "Loren?"

"Yes?" She turned, one hand on the knob.

"When January the first comes, if you find you'll need a longer rest, just give me a call and we'll arrange it for you."

Plans for a Journey

"That's extremely kind of you, Mr. Adson, but I'll do my best to get back." She nodded and closed the door gently.

The week flew by now, for she found so much to do in preparation for leaving. Finally, with her ticket purchased and tucked safely in her purse, she called Cathy.

"Guess what, Cathy?"

"I don't know, but from the sound of your voice I'd say it's good news."

"I'm leaving Saturday for Manitoba."

"You're kidding me!"

"No, honestly! I'm all packed, and everything's arranged right down to my ticket."

"But. . .well, I mean, shouldn't you arrange to have someone meet you there, or something? It is a strange place and. . .oh, you know!"

"And who would you suggest?" Loren couldn't control the sarcasm in her voice.

"Well," Cathy made an uncertain sound, "I guess perhaps you are in a difficult position for that."

"Right! Seeing as how I don't know anyone. But don't worry. There's bound to be a hotel or motel or someplace to hang my hat. After all, it is a town!"

"But Loren, try to be a little more. . .uh. . .oh, what shall I call it? Aggressive, I guess. You've been so. . .so. . .withdrawn or something lately."

"Don't worry about me, Cathy. Now that I've made up my mind, it's a quest I have to pursue!"

"Well, I wish you all the best in the world, Loren. I just wish you weren't going so far away. Be sure to keep in touch!"

"I will. You and John and Hazel are really the only

'family' I have now, and I'm not apt to forget you. Anyway, I plan to be back the first of the year. Have a good Christmas without me. Personally, I think I'll just forget about Christmas."

"Be sure to let us know when you uncover a relative, Loren."

"I sure will, and I hope it's a speedy process!"

"What time is your flight out Saturday?"

"It's 11:30 p.m. Can you believe it? I'll be traveling all night."

"That's not so bad. Just be sure to get some sleep so you'll be rested and keen for your project."

"No problem. At this point, I think I've let my problem obsess me. There are times I just wish I could ask Dad a few questions. . . ." Her voice trailed off.

"Don't torment yourself with thoughts like that, Loren. Try to keep your mind off that angle. Hey, we'll be out to the airport to see you off Saturday night, or maybe we could even take you there. Do you have a ride?"

"But it's too late, Cathy! You don't have to do that. I'll take a taxi."

"You mean you prefer a cab to your friends? You won't need to do that! We'll pick you up. What time would you like us to be there?"

"Oh, Cathy. . ."

"We'll be there at 10:30. That's what friends are for, you know!"

"But you've already done more than your share!"

As Loren hung up the telephone, a sudden wave of excitement engulfed her. She was actually going to Manitoba to seek for her roots! Then apprehension struck. If she was successful in her search for yesterday, what would she discover about her past? Whom would she find, and what would they be like?

CHAPTER

7

Flight West

It was Loren's first lengthy flight. Because of a snowstorm there was some delay so her plane had to land unexpectedly in Minneapolis. The airline took care of the necessary arrangements, and Loren was relieved to get a good rest, for she had not been able to sleep in flight. The four-hour delay meant that she would reach her destination late Monday afternoon. She wondered briefly if this would make it more difficult to find a room for the night, as she had not made any advance arrangements. Her search for information had turned up very little, except that Neuberg was a small town of about four thousand people.

Her uneasiness grew as the plane's captain gave them landing details. "We are approaching our destination. Within thirty minutes we will be touching down at Brandon, Manitoba. There are six small towns within an hour's radius of the city: Minnedosa, Neuberg, Carberry, Virden,

Souris and Rivers."

Aside from following his instructions to fasten her seat belt, Loren paid little attention to the pilot's remarks. Her preoccupation with what might await her caused a queasy feeling to grab at her stomach even before they began the descent.

She stood off to one side after alighting, feeling alone and uncertain as other passengers were greeted and clasped by waiting friends and relatives. She fixed her gaze on the luggage belt without really seeing it, only to be alerted with a start by the announcement of a flight departure time. She was going to have to move if she planned on reaching Neuberg before sundown!

A blue bag came toward her on the luggage belt, and she bent to retrieve it. A man on her left had the same idea, and their heads came together with a resounding crack. Loren straightened up, dizzy and without the bag, but the man quickly passed it to her.

"Sorry! Are you all right?"

She nodded mutely.

"I thought this was mine," he added quickly, "but I see it's not. Can I get you a cab?"

"Thanks, but I'll look after it." She snatched the bag and moved swiftly, though unsteadily, in the direction of the public telephones. By the time the cab arrived she had regained her composure and deftness and wondered what the stranger must have thought of her reaction. Her face burned as she realized she had acted rather stunned—but then she actually had been rather stunned, and it wasn't all her fault.

The cab driver tapped his fingers impatiently on the dash while he waited for her response to his "Where to,

Flight West

ma'am?"

"Oh. . .uh. . .make it Neuberg. Is that very far from here?"

"No, a half-hour's drive when the roads are good. They've been plowed, but they could be a good deal better. We just had a foot or so of snow, so they're all snow-packed."

He seemed an amicable fellow so she pushed her luck. "I've never been to Neuberg before. Are you familiar with the town?"

"Know it like the back of my hand. Lived there in my teens."

Loren's heart gave a lurch. "I suppose you know most folks in the area?"

"I'd have to say I did know most folks. There's been a population turnover there in the past few years; all the oldtimers have gone off the scene. Used to be a mining town at one time but the place is fast becoming a ghost town. Mined out, I guess. Oh, they still have the staid old family names like the McDonalds . . . Guenthers . . . Smiths. . .Oultons. They'll never leave the place, but more recent families have come and gone. Moved on to the next mining town. A lot of the miners are that way. They follow the job from one place to the next."

"Did you ever hear of a family. . .named Schmitt?" She held her breath.

"No. . .oo, can't say I did."

Loren sighed disappointedly and sat back in the seat. So much for that she thought. Another false lead.

They soon approached the town and the speed limit changed. A row of small shade trees sheltered a park area. The fountain sparkled under a layer of new-fallen snow, and the barren tree boughs bowed beneath their load of snowy diamonds. The late afternoon sun cast long shadows on the unbroken expanse of whiteness. In spite of the frigidity the scene conveyed, Loren caught her breath at the splendorous sight.

"And this is Neuberg! I love the way the powdery snow seems to twinkle back at everything."

"Yes, It is a pretty sight, but it can sure be a nuisance—and cold at that!" He turned to face her. "What address, Miss?"

"Uh. . .well. . .is there a hotel or rooming house in town?"

"There is a small hotel, but they tell me it's not up to par where cleanliness is concerned. You didn't arrange for a place to go?"

"I'm afraid not. I was hoping. . . ."

"Don't worry," he interrupted. "We'll fix you up in no time. Miss Claire takes in roomers on a limited-time basis, though she does have two permanent residents. At least you could get a place there for tonight. She has a big old house with plenty of room, and most people don't stay around there too long."

"Well, I can't say I'd relish staying out of doors in this weather." She laughed with just a hint of a quiver in her voice.

"You might be ready to stay outside after a day or so of Miss Claire's prying. She can be an awful nuisance at times."

Loren, unsure of what he was trying to tell her, merely managed an uncertain "Oh?"

"Yup! Small town gossip. She makes it a hobby; nothin' else to do, I guess."

Loren laughed in relief. "Oh, I think I can handle that!"

"Sure! Put her in her place! I'd like to see someone do it. No one deserves it more than she does."

Once Loren stood in the hallway of the big old house, being scrutinized by the overpowering Miss Claire, she was no longer so sure of her ability to handle the situation. Anyway, she had a room for tonight. Tomorrow, she would look for another.

CHAPTER

8

Encounter with Miss Claire

Loren awoke to strange surroundings and for a moment could not get her bearings. Snow was falling past the window and the dark, unimaginative furnishings filled the room with a sense of gloom. Then she remembered. Ah! Neuberg!

As the clock in the town hall struck seven, she recalled Miss Claire's parting words of the night before. "Most of the guests are around by seven, except for the occasional lazy one who likes to spend half the day in bed."

Loren threw back the covers and scurried about. At 7:20 she emerged from the bath and proceeded downstairs, only to confront Miss Claire's half scowl in the lower hall.

"Well, I see you're up and about. I serve breakfast at 7:30. The dining room is the second door down, past

In Search Of Yesterday

the main entry."

She continued up the stairs, apparently to arouse a "lazy" guest, and Loren made her way to the dining area. A cluster of guests were talking animatedly as she entered, stopping only briefly to glance her way then resuming the conversation. No one was seated, so she assumed they waited for Miss Claire's return. They hadn't long to wait. It was as though Loren's conscious thought had conjured up the unpleasant image. Immediately the hum drum ceased, and the announcement was made: "You might as well be seated. Mr. Dickson is passing breakfast by in favor of sleep." She sniffed haughtily. "Looks like that party last night was to his detriment."

Loren waited to be seated, not wishing to take another's chair, and Miss Claire merely pointed to a vacancy for both her and another guest who seemed to be a stranger to the group. Loren was relieved that Miss Claire was not the cook, for she felt almost certain the food would spoil under the woman's gaze of displeasure. She was doubly glad that the others were not directing conversation to her, for she preferred to remain silent. She should have realized that she could not remain in that state forever.

Miss Claire herself was soon at her elbow, asking a question she would have preferred to ignore. "And where do you hail from, Miss Neilson?"

"I come from the east coast of Canada."

"And just what particular place?"

"New Brunswick."

"You don't say! I once had a friend from New Brunswick; Moore was the name. Don't suppose you know a Duncan Moore?"

Loren was tempted to laugh but didn't dare. What was wrong with these people? They had such a limited concept of New Brunswick, or Canada for that matter, that they thought everyone there should know everyone else. She managed to answer in a serious tone. "I'm afraid I've never met him. In fact, I don't believe I ever made the acquaintance of a single Moore, though I'm familiar with the name."

"I take it you've been rather limited in your traveling."

"Yes, I'm afraid so." Loren smiled. She didn't intend to feed her any more information than necessary.

"I suppose you're here to see a friend?" She put slight emphasis on the word friend.

"Nothing of the sort."

"Oh? Then what are you here for?"

"I'm doing some research," she answered stiffly.

"And in what field, may I ask?"

Inwardly, Loren seethed, but outwardly she put on her sweetest smile, looked her directly in the eye and answered the question. "Of course, you may ask, but I may not disclose. It's of a secret nature."

Conversation had stopped the length of the table, and Loren could feel the inquisitive eyes turned in her direction. Hurriedly she finished her coffee and excused herself. She felt a sense of triumph, even though embarrassed, and could sense Miss Claire's indignant displeasure following her out the door.

Hastily she packed up her belongings. She had to find another rooming house!

Miss Claire had her back turned, talking to a number of guests, as Loren came down the stairs. Her words carried to Loren. "I don't believe it! There's something strange about such behavior, and I intend to find out what's going on. She needn't think she can escape attention in this small town! I'll have her number before the day ends."

Uh, sorry to disturb you, Miss Claire, but I think I'll be going on my way now."

"You mean. . .You're going back east?"

"Oh, no. But I do need a permanent place to stay."

"Well, you could stay here, you know; certainly until my guests from Oregon arrive at the end of this week. And I can tell you now—you won't find another place. Lil Smith takes roomers, but I happen to know she's full up at the moment!"

"What about the hotel?"

"My dear! That's no place for a young lady of repute! Especially on a permanent basis." At Loren's downcast expression, she added, "I think you'd best stay here for the time, Miss Neilsen. Maybe next week Lil Smith can take you in."

"Well, perhaps I could leave my bags here. . .just for now. . .but I think I'll go take a look around anyway." Loren started reluctantly up the stairs. Silence followed her.

In the room, she set the suitcase down and threw herself across the bed, a great aching loneliness overwhelming her. She managed to squeeze back the tears, but a rending sob shook her body. What was she doing here anyway? She was on a fool's errand! Although she missed her father terribly, she knew there was nothing she could do about it. On the other hand, she could have chosen to remain near her friends awhile. Oh! If Cathy were only here! Or Hazel! But they weren't so she would have to conjure up someone who could share this load with her.

There must be someone she could turn to in this little town. The thought intruded in spite of her gloom. What if there actually was a relative in this place? Within walking distance, maybe! The thought spurred her on. There was only one way to find out, and that's what she had come for. She got up and washed her face, then walked resolutely past the "Miss Claire forum" at the foot of the stairs.

"See you later," she smiled as she went out the door.

CHAPTER

9

A Visit to Neuberg Town Hall

The snowflakes were big and sparse, and Loren concluded that there was no real threat of a storm as she walked casually to the street corner. Once there, she hadn't the slightest idea of which direction to take to find the town hall, although she attempted to give the appearance of being familiar with her surroundings. The letter Cathy had received from Neuberg Town Hall was in her purse. After hunting a few seconds she managed to come up with it, but in vain, for it merely said, "Neuberg Town Hall," followed by a catchy slogan.

Loren supposed she could have asked Miss Claire, but there was just no way her pride would allow her to glean information from that busybody. Abruptly she thrust the letter back in her handbag, and just as abruptly, the clock at Town Hall struck the hour. Loren listened, then turned in the direction of the sound—northwest. Within two blocks of the old building, she could see the clock tower.

She hadn't passed a single individual in the last six blocks, but somehow she got the impression of curtains being pushed sneakily aside as she passed. Without doubt, this old town nosily observed every newcomer with silent tolerance.

The steps of the hall were piled with snow. It looked as if no one had been there in weeks. Keenly disappointed, Loren was about to turn and leave when a breathless young man came hurrying along with a shovel.

"Just give me a minute. Sorry I'm late, but I had to go back for this," he explained, indicating the shovel. "I forgot that no one bothers to clear the snow when I'm absent." He soon had a clear walk and proceeded to turn the key in the heavy, old brass lock.

It took a few minutes to become accustomed to the dark interior, but even when the lights were on the place was dark and gloomy.

The man hurried behind a cluttered desk and began to clear off the debris. "I've been away," he offered apologetically. "Just got home last night, and nobody's been in to clean up for me. Now, what can I do for you?" His task finished, he looked directly at her. "Hey! Haven't we met before. . .somewhere?"

Loren stared in disbelief. Oh no! Not him! It was the young man of yesterday who had given her head a bump. She stammered, hoping he'd forget where. "No. . .no! I don't believe I've ever met you."

The young man laughed and extended his hand. "For a minute there, I was sure I had seen you somewhere. Well, I'm Ted Armor—City Hall Manager, for what the title's worth. Actually, I guess you could say I'm a records clerk and file keeper."

Loren managed a smile in response. "I'm Loren. . . Loren Neilsen."

"I don't think that's a strange name to this town. Used to be Neilsens in the area, though the last one moved some years ago. And what can I do for you, Miss. . .is it Miss Neilsen?"

She nodded. "Actually, I'm here as a result of this letter." Loren passed him the piece of correspondence.

"Oh, sure, I remember now. You're trying to locate someone."

"Right. I wouldn't mind finding any relative, but I thought it might be best to start with the individual in the letter."

"Elizabett Schmitt?"

"I have reason to believe she's my grandmother."

"Well, let's have a look. I recall pulling that file, and I think there were only a few certificates. I believe she must have moved. Let's see now. Where is that?" He proceeded to pull the file from the "S" listing and brought it for her to examine.

She glanced at the forms, disappointed. "I. . .I have most of this. . .except for her birth certificate. This is all?"

"I'm afraid so. We have no death certificate for her, so she must be living somewhere. All I can imagine is that she must have moved away. She's listed as 'Elizabett (Betty) Schmitt.' I've lived here all my life and have yet to hear of a Betty Schmitt."

The door of the hall opened, and a tall graying gentleman came breezily in.

"Hello there, Doctor Olsen!"

"Hi, Ted. It's good to see you back again. I haven't had a leisurely conversation break for two weeks. Thought I'd stop by."

"Sure! Sure! I'm glad you've come by. Say, Doc, maybe you could help this little lady. Seeing as how you've been around longer than I have, you'd know people before my time. Ever hear of Elizabett Schmitt?"

"Elizabett...Elizabett...why, yes, Ted. I have. And I don't suppose anyone in the community would know her better than Miss Claire."

"You mean the town gossip?" Loren dispensed with tact.

"Well, I like to think of her as the general information file for our town. But then, all the old-timers know who Betty Schmitt is!" He looked at Loren. "And what's your name, young lady?"

Before she could answer, the door was thrust open behind them, and someone called in alarm, "Come quick, Doctor Olsen! Your house is on fire!"

With giant strides the doctor was out the door, into his automobile, and speeding away before Ted and Loren began to react. As they ran into the street, the sky was brilliantly lit against the dark curtain of an impending storm. They stood in shock for a minute before Ted spoke, almost inaudibly.

"It must be gone by the looks of things. That house is on the other side of town."

CHAPTER 10

In Search of Betty Schmitt

Miss Claire was full of news about the fire. Loren looked at her with disgust. She actually seemed to thrive on that sort of thing. She has to gossip in order to survive, Loren thought as she hurried up the stairs. She wasn't about to stay and hear her gloat about how she got the facts. To be honest, she resented staying in the woman's presence another day, but where could she go?

The lunch gong sounded, and Loren reluctantly made her way downstairs. She realized that if she really wanted information about her family, in all likelihood Miss Claire could provide it. Pride kept her from asking, for along with the facts, Miss Claire would find it necessary to repeat all the gossip, or "inside info," as she liked to call it. No, she didn't want to hear anything from Miss Claire!

As Loren descended the steps, a cold draft crept up

In Search Of Yesterday

the steps from the open doorway, where Miss Claire was asking, "Have you heard, Lil? About the fire, I mean?" The elderly lady on the sidewalk paused just a minute.

"Yes. A terrible thing, Claire! Poor Doc Olsen! Now he'll really need prayer!"

"Humph!" Claire slammed the door and came back in muttering aloud, "That's all she ever thinks of!"

"And who's that?" One of the guests asked impertinently.

"Oh, that's Lil Smith! Too bad she hadn't thought of prayer for her own clan, but I doubt it would have done any good!"

"Are you speaking of Bob Smith's mother?"

"Who else?" Her voice was full of contempt.

"Well, I've met Bob, and he's an A-1 guy. It must have done him some good."

"At one time Lil was OK too. She was a good friend of mine, but that's certainly changed."

Disgruntled, Miss Claire huffed her way out to the kitchen to vent her ire on the cook.

Loren had managed to get a glimpse of the old lady on the sidewalk, and there was something pleasant about her appearance. That must be the same Lil Smith who had the rooming house, she concluded. She should go see her this afternoon. Maybe she'd have a room after all. There was no harm in trying.

Soup and sandwich finished, Loren got into her outside apparel and ventured out into the gray afternoon. A few flurries of snow were still falling, and Loren was as uncertain as before about which way to go. For a moment she was tempted to swallow her pride, retrace her steps and ask Miss Claire how to get to Lil Smith's.

In Search of Betty Schmitt

"Oh fie!" she scolded herself. "Why must I have so much pride?" Without realizing it, Loren started walking in the direction of Town Hall and arguing with herself as she walked. "No, it's not pride; it's only self-respect. No nosy, prying busybody is going to interfere in my affairs." Mulling over the matter, she glanced up at her surroundings, recognized the hall and hurried on by. From now on, she would take more care of where she was going. After all, she would need to find her way back again. She should have been paying attention.

Just ahead a sign hung over the street. She stopped, amazed as she read the inscription: "Dr. A. Olsen, M.D." This was the office of the doctor she had met this morning. He would no doubt be back by the first of next week. Things would be simple from here on. He said he knew Betty Schmitt. She wouldn't need Miss Claire's help.

More lighthearted than she had been in weeks, Loren turned back in the direction she had come. Now, if someone would only tell her where Lil Smith's boarding house was, she felt certain that things would work out. Just as she had gone beyond Town Hall, she heard someone call her name. In seconds, Ted Armor had fallen in step.

"Looks like we might be going in the same direction. Where are you staying?"

"At Miss Claire's."

"Oh, really?" He glanced at her sympathetically. "You really should have tried Lil Smith's."

"Well, her name was mentioned to me, and to be truthful with you, that's why I've been out walking. I've been hoping to come across her place."

"Why didn't you ask Miss Claire about it? She knows where everyone lives. Actually, Lil's just about six blocks

In Search Of Yesterday

beyond Town Hall. Go up two blocks till you come to Doc Olsen's office, then turn left and go south four more. It's a big yellow house with a glassed-in porch. There are some huge oak trees on the front lawn—the only place like it on that block."

"Oh, thanks so much! I guess I should have asked but. . .well. . .I don't like prying individuals and. . ." She stopped, and he laughingly finished the thought for her.

"So you were reluctant to set yourself up for questioning."

Loren slowed her walk. "Perhaps I should go there now. . .to this Miss or Mrs. Smith's. . .whatever. . ."

"It's Mrs. And I have a better idea. You'll notice I'm leaving work early. I don't normally leave midafternoon, but I have some work to do—a sermon to prepare, in fact. You see, tonight is young people's night at our church, and Bob Smith asked me to speak. He's our young people's leader, and a son of the boarding house lady. So. . .if you'll come with me to church. . ."

"Oh, I couldn't," she interrupted. "I haven't been to church since. . .since Dad's funeral."

"Sorry. Was it recently?"

She merely nodded, timid of threatening tears.

"Then I'm truly sorry. But really, if you want to see Lil Smith, she's sure to be at church, and if not, Bob can take you to her."

"It seems to me it would be much simpler to turn and go back there now."

"Not really. First of all, you've walked almost across town this afternoon, and that's enough for one day, but more importantly, Lil would not be home. Tuesday and Friday are her shopping days, so you probably wouldn't

In Search of Betty Schmitt

catch her until just about suppertime. It seems to me your safest bet would be to come along to church and talk to the lady there."

Reluctantly, Loren consented. She had to have a place to stay. On the other hand, she had no desire to get involved with religion. It had never had a place in her life, and as far as she was concerned, she had never missed it. Neither was she anxious to get mixed up with some religious nut. She was just a bit leery of this Armor guy. He sounded like he might be on the borderline. Oh, well, she wouldn't need to get involved, and if Lil Smith were there, her problem would be solved.

"Well, this is where I live." Ted's voice brought her back to her surroundings. "Would you like me to walk you to Miss Claire's?"

"No! Oh, no! It's just a short way."

"You won't get lost?"

She shook her head and smiled a reply.

"I've covered the area a few times now. I'll do fine. Besides, I'm sure Miss Claire has had her quota of gossip for one day. Can you imagine what would happen if a young man accompanied me to her door?"

"Sure can! We'll save that for tonight when I come to pick you up for church. See you later!"

Distressed, Loren barely heard his last words as she mulled over how to avoid Miss Claire's scrutiny this evening.

CHAPTER

11

Another Boarding House

Loren went straight to her room, ignoring Miss Claire's attempts at conversation. She could think of no legitimate way to get past her interrogation again tonight. There was bound to be a confrontation, for Miss Claire would be sure to inquire about her wanderings if she left early, as she had thought she might do. On the other hand, if Ted came by, as she presumed he would, it would certainly spark Miss Claire's curiosity, and there would be no getting around the subject.

"Miss Neilsen! Yahoo, Miss Neilsen! Telephone!"

Loren hurried down the stairs to where her hostess held the telephone at arm's length.

She was smiling smugly. "Well, this is a surprise! I do believe it's Ted Armor asking for you."

Loren took the phone reluctantly, realizing her scheming attempts to keep Ted out of the picture were in vain. She barely heard what he was saying as she waited for

In Search Of Yesterday

Miss Claire to leave the room. As she became aware the latter had no such intentions, she condensed her answers to monosyllables and hung up as soon as possible. At least, she understood he was coming for her at 6:30.

Turning hastily toward the stairs, she attempted to get away from Miss Claire's prying eyes and knowing smile. "You might as well stay down, Miss Neilsen. Supper's just about ready." A half smile twitched at her mouth. "And if you'd like any information on Ted Armor, I could probably help you as much as anyone."

Loren gave her a cold stare. "Thanks, but I won't be eating dinner tonight." She hurried back to her room, trembling with indignation at the old woman's implications. She barely knew Ted Armor! Now what would the town be hearing from that old windbag?

She pulled a favorite dress from her bag and zipped herself into it, then combed her auburn waves into place. She began to stuff her belongings into her blue case and pulled the zipper with unnecessary gusto. Church or no church! She didn't care where she was going! She was leaving here. She'd sleep in a snowdrift on the sidewalk first!

The smell of baked ham drifted up the stairs and she was suddenly ravenous, but there was just no way that she would subject herself to an interrogation over supper. If she could not get into Lil Smith's, she would insist that Ted take her to that hotel. Any place would be better than this! Loren sat on the bed, her luggage at her feet, and seethed inwardly until she heard the sound of the doorbell. Rather than wait for Miss Claire's call, she grabbed her bags and bolted down the stairs, halting halfway at the sound of Miss Claire's probing.

"Why, you never told us a thing about this, Ted! Why be so secretive?"

"About what, Miss Claire?"

"Miss Neilsen. What else? The whole town's been curious about those trips you were taking. Why, you even went to New Brunswick, did you not?"

"I'm afraid I don't follow you, Miss Claire. Miss Neilsen has had nothing to do with my business trips."

"Come now!"

"Miss Claire!" Loren could keep still no longer. "Mr. Armor and I have only recently met!" She struggled to control her surge of anger as she pushed her way past. "I'll not be back tonight. I'm getting a new boarding place."

Miss Claire sniffed haughtily. "Well, wherever you decided to stay, I hope it's reputable!"

Loren, white with anger, chose not to respond, but Ted actually laughed as he reached for her luggage and closed the door behind them. "Hey! I didn't realize you'd be taking this to church. I thought you'd be getting a place, then come back for your bags."

"And face more of that? No way! I'll not darken that door again!"

"Well, had I known, I would have had Bob come by with the car."

"Oh! You don't have a car? I guess I just never thought to ask. How far do we have to walk?"

"No distance really. A block and a half, but this case is getting heavy. I don't know how you've been lugging it around, especially up and down those stairs."

"Well, I was so mad back there I could have lugged it clear across town. I just can't stand that prying old woman!"

"Oh, she doesn't mean any harm. Around here, everyone accepts her role as village gossip. Frankly though, I don't know how anyone could stay there. Most people stay overnight, but she does have two permanent guests—elderly folks who either don't care what she has to say or simply ignore her. I don't know, perhaps they enjoy the gossip as much as she does. Beats me how they put up with her."

They reached the church, and Ted set the bag beneath the coat rack in the vestibule. Hesitantly, Loren followed him inside. They were met at the door of the auditorium by a strikingly handsome young man who shook hands warmly as introductions were made. Loren's thoughts swirled. So this was Bob Smith! And he seemed so friendly! It was enough to quicken any girl's pulse. She hoped his mother was half as nice as he. Would she be comfortable living in the same house as this charming young fellow? She forced herself back to the conversation at hand.

"Have you tried Miss Claire's?" Bob asked.

"Miss Claire's! Are you serious?" She hadn't intended to sound so rude, but Ted laughingly explained for her.

"Bob, this lady is attempting to escape Miss Claire's! Can you believe it?"

"Oh, oh! Then I did detect a note of hostility in her reply."

Both men laughed heartily, and Bob suggested that Ted introduce Loren to his mother, "Although," he added quickly, "I'm not sure there's a room at the present time."

With a start, Loren realized Bob's mother was the

Another Boarding House

same Lil Smith she had glimpsed on the sidewalk talking to Miss Claire about Doctor Olsen. She looked tiny and stooped and much too old to have a son so young. Apparently, she was also a widow, for no one had mentioned Bob's father, and she was alone. Loren found her every bit as charming as her son. She had the same smiling black eyes, but her hair was combed in soft puffs of gray braid which she had twined together in a tidy bun in back. She was petite and fragile-looking as well as quick-witted and friendly, and she put Loren at ease at once. Loren could feel the elderly woman's sympathy extend to her as Ted explained her predicament.

"I'm sorry about this problem with Miss Claire, and I truly wish I could help, but—until Friday, that is, we're booked up. There will be a vacancy at that time."

"The problem is right now. Where does she go tonight?"

Loren could scarcely keep her disappointment from showing. "I suppose I could go to the hotel. . ."

"Oh, my dear, I'd rather you didn't! It really isn't a very respectable place. Just a minute. . .Ted, get Bob for me, will you?"

By the time Bob arrived, it appeared he had been informed. "Yes, Mother. I know what you're thinking. And yes! For the umpteenth time, I'll sleep on the sofa until Mr. Spear leaves."

"Oh, I wouldn't want to take anyone's bed! Why, I'm sure I can take care of myself. I'll go along to the hotel."

Bob threw back his shoulders and attempted to look fierce. "Nothing doing! Over my dead body! If it will help any, this is something I'm doing for my mother as well as you. I do this sort of thing all the time—just for Mother.

In Search Of Yesterday

Right, Mom?"

Mrs. Smith smiled and gave his hand a squeeze. "Then it's settled. Miss Neilsen, you may come home with me."

"Thank you! But I do hate to take your son's bed!"

"You won't be. You can take Mr. Spear's and he will take Bob's. He'll be leaving on Friday anyway, so Bob will have his room back soon. And if he doesn't mind, you shouldn't."

"I. . .I do appreciate this. Thanks a lot!"

"You're more than welcome. Now, why don't you stay right here with me for service. I'm sure you'll enjoy it. I wouldn't miss young people's service for the world. I'm still young at heart, you know," she laughed.

Loren managed a half smile in reply. Her own discomfort at being in church was all too obvious. I hope, she thought, that she is right about my enjoying this service, but I'm not so sure! Mentally, she prepared herself to reject what she was about to hear.

Actually, there were not too many older folks in attendance, aside from the few who Loren thought must be the youth's parents. What did surprise her was the number of teen-agers there. She had never been a regular churchgoer, but neither had any of the other youth where she had spent her teen years.

CHAPTER

12

Introduction to Church

This, to Loren, was unlike any church service she had never attended. Not only was Lil Smith's singing exuberant, the young people sang with such enthusiasm that it fascinated their visitor. Though she hadn't really wanted to come and had no intentions of participating, she soon found herself humming along with them.

Loren found it a bit difficult to keep her eyes off the extremely handsome youth leader. Vaguely, she was reminded briefly of her past engagement but attempted to push the thought quickly aside. It really hadn't been all her fault the way things had happened. She just needed time to think, but obviously Jim had been ready for marriage, so he simply found someone else. Yes, this Smith chap did remind her of Jim. When she felt the dull ache of reminiscence, she did her best to concentrate on what Bob was saying.

"There is such assurance to be found in Christ—such

In Search Of Yesterday

security and joy."

He could say that! He probably had never had his world crumble around him. He still had his mother and, no doubt, other family members. It appeared that she had given him anything he desired. He was obviously an only son. He could feel secure in a way that Loren was sure she never could—secure in the love of a family.

Bob Smith asked for testimonies, and to her amazement, a number of youth stood, surprising Loren with their testimonies about the same sort of joy Bob had spoken of. Loren was sure there would be no joy in life for her, unless she could locate Elizabett Schmitt. It was becoming almost an obsession. Even if she couldn't find her grandmother, any member of the family would do. She needed a family—a sense of belonging and completeness. She'd gladly accept any relative she could locate. Then, perhaps, she would find happiness and joy.

Loren's concentration was broken when Lil Smith stood to her feet. She testified with an intensity that Loren found disturbing. For a minute Loren felt a compulsion to get up and leave. Her last wish was to get entangled with a group of zealots. The elderly lady's words suddenly stopped her thoughts cold as her voice rose in a crescendo.

"I realize none of you young people know where the Lord has brought me from. It was long before your time. Let me tell you, I hit rock bottom! I had family problems and had sunk in utter despair, but Christ reached down and lifted me to a higher plane. Miss Claire and I were the best of friends at that time, but she chose to go a different way. In fact, Miss Claire gave me the nickname of Lil. She said I was not the friend she used to know and

I didn't deserve my old name, so Lil I became. And, you know, when I think about it, I realize I really wasn't the old friend she had known for years. I was a new person—a new creation in Christ Jesus, and the new name suited me fine.

"I'm so glad I made the decision to follow the Lord. What a difference it's made in my life! He really is the answer to all of life's problems."

She sat down and wiped a lace-edged handkerchief across her brow. Loren wondered if such fervor were really a healthy thing and, for a moment, almost expected the old lady to collapse. But, as she found out in just a few minutes, she really hadn't heard anything yet, for Ted Armor's message was the icing on the cake.

Ted spoke with a sincerity that even Loren found hard to discredit. He recapitulated everything the others had said, but he also made the plan of salvation so clear that Loren was once again struggling with the desire to leave—to get up and walk out of this fervently religious group and their persuasive tactics. Maybe she should have stayed at Miss Claire's after all. How would she ever fit in at Lil Smith's? Actually, she wished for the second time in as many days that she had stayed in New Brunswick.

Ted asked the congregation to stand for dismissal, and Loren stood up with a great sense of relief. At least, they would be out of this atmosphere!

As she followed Lil Smith to the car, she was embarrassed to find they didn't actually have room for another passenger. She hadn't thought about that! But Bob insisted there was always room for one more.

"No trouble at all! Why, this car has seen more people than this inside. We've often squeezed in passengers until the doors would scarcely close." And he launched into the tale of some past episode when the car was stopped by police for being so overcrowded. Loren listened and laughed with everyone else, her embarrassment subsiding.

CHAPTER

13

Pleasant Surroundings

The guest room that Mr. Spear was occupying had to be vacated, and since he was out for the evening, they could do nothing but sit and wait for his return.

Lil Smith made coffee while they waited. As they sat around the dining room table, much to Loren's chagrin Mrs. Smith asked the same question Miss Claire had asked about where she came from. As she explained briefly, the older woman seemed genuinely interested in her background. Loren was tempted to ask her about Elizabett Schmitt, but something—probably her being a friend of Miss Claire's—held her back.

"You do have a name that was once familiar to these parts. Neilsen used to be one of the early settler's names in this area. Unfortunately, they've all moved away, and the name has died out here." She stopped talking and a faraway look of sadness clouded her eyes. Loren was about to ask if she had personally known any Neilsens,

In Search Of Yesterday

when the door opened and in sauntered Mr. Spear.

Lil Smith made introductions and explained the situation. The stately gentleman was more than willing to cooperate. He moved his things into Bob's room, and Bob put Loren's suitcase in the vacated room.

"Thank you, Bob!" Loren smiled prettily, and the light from the open doorway made a halo of her auburn locks.

"You are very welcome, Miss Neilsen!"

"Please call me Loren."

"All right, Loren. It's not often we are privileged to have such a beautiful young lady as our guest for any length of time. Usually Miss Claire captures them first, and after two or three days they're ready to leave town. I'm glad you've come."

Loren's heart did a flip. Flustered, she wasn't sure she should respond further, so she simply stepped into the hallway and called to her hostess, "Good night. I've had a terribly long day, and I think I'm ready to retire."

"An unpleasant day also, I suppose," the older lady added.

Loren smiled at Bob. "Good night, Bob. I'm so relieved I found a place to stay."

"So am I. Good night." He turned and was gone. Loren closed the door and sat down on the side of the bed. She had been weary, but somewhere in that exchange the weariness had seeped away.

"Loren," she scolded herself, "don't you dare set your cap for some religious nut!"

The scolding didn't help much. Even after she changed into her night clothes and fell into bed, her mind was a carousel of conflicting thoughts.

70

Pleasant Surroundings

Sleep came slowly, but at last she drifted into a disturbing dream. In her dream she scurried about Neuberg looking for Elizabett Schmitt. Bob and Ted were both trying to help, but each gave different directions, frustrating her efforts even further. At last she rushed away from them and began running toward Miss Claire's. Miss Claire would help her. Miss Claire knew everyone. To her disgust and amazement, she found herself back on Lil Smith's doorstep. She would have turned and taken up her pursuit once more, but Bob and Ted came into view. She decided to wait until tomorrow to make her way to Miss Claire's. Once the mind had settled that issue, she slept more soundly.

CHAPTER

14

An Unpleasant Topic

Because she had not been able to go directly to sleep the night before, Loren was late in rising. What would Mrs. Smith say? If her reaction should happen to be anything like Miss Claire's, Loren determined she would set out for home at once.

Her room had its own bath, and for that she was grateful. At least, she wouldn't need to confront the other guests for a while. And what time was breakfast? They had failed to tell her, and she had forgotten to ask. Although she was reluctant to emerge from her room, she knew she had no choice but to answer when she heard a knock at her door.

It was Bob, dressed to go out. "Mother heard you and sent me to tell you breakfast will be ready anytime you'd like to have it." His smile was disarming.

Loren stammered a response. Afterward, she was not sure what she had said, but she guessed it must have been acceptable as he left without further ado.

Lil Smith met her in the dining room doorway with a pot of freshly-made coffee.

"Sorry I'm late!" Loren stammered. "I guess I didn't realize just how tired I was."

"Don't worry your pretty head about it! There have been times when I've had to awaken guests to catch a train, or a flight out or something, but unless they asked to be aroused early they could sleep all day around here. I had no intentions of waking you this morning as I knew you were exhausted when you retired. If you do need to get up early, for an appointment or some other reason, just leave word the night before. Bob's always around early, so one of us could call you."

"But I'm afraid I've inconvenienced you this morning with getting breakfast and all."

Lil waved a hand at her in dismissal of the idea. "Nothing to it! I've done things this way all my life. People are my business. I kept your waffles hot, and I'd do the same for anyone."

She went to the kitchen and returned with a plate of steaming waffles and a pitcher of syrup. "There you go, and I'm going to sit down with you for my midmorning coffee." As though she read Loren's mind, she went on, "Bob's gone out for the day. He works at the church office most mornings and goes to his own office in the afternoon. He's a chartered accountant downtown. Actually, there's not a great deal of work in this town, so he gives his extra hours to church work. And I'm glad! The church is always needing volunteers."

"Volunteers?" Loren looked at her aghast. "You mean he doesn't get paid for spending his mornings at

An Unpleasant Topic

the church office?"

"No. Since he's not busy at anything else, it gives him something to do. He sometimes helps me here with the guest house in the morning when other work gets slack, and then he goes over there."

"But you'd think they'd pay!"

"Oh, they would! He just doesn't expect it. He gives of his time to the Lord's work out of appreciation for what the Lord has given him."

"I see," Loren said a little too quickly, though she really didn't. She wanted to steer the conversation away from the topic of religion, which was obviously where it was headed.

Later, as Loren came out of her room dressed to go out, Mrs. Smith had a suggestion. "Perhaps you'd rather wait for Bob to come home, my dear, and let him show you around the town this evening."

"I. . .I appreciate that, but I do have something to do, and I really need to get at it now. Besides, I've been around town a bit, and I'm sure I can find my way all right."

"Well, whatever you think. I imagine by the way Ted Armor was looking at you that he'd be more than happy to show you around, too."

Loren blushed. Reminders of Miss Claire! "We've barely met and that was purely by accident!"

"Sorry! No offense intended! I just couldn't help but notice. And Ted is such a fine Christian fellow. Doesn't have a steady girlfriend now, either."

A fine Christian fellow I do not need, Loren thought, but aloud she said, "I think I ought to go now. I came here strictly on business, and too many late mornings and too much loitering won't get my business done."

In her mind she continued, "And why, may I ask do you seem to think I need a fellow at all? I am doing perfectly well by myself. Incompetence has never been my classification. In fact, on the job I'm known as the individual who gets the job done."

Loren was unaware that her pace of walking quickened as her anger intensified. Letting her imagination work her into a nasty frame of mind, she began to fume inside. Just once, she decided, she would have liked to come back with the first retort that came to her mind. Had it been Miss Claire, she could have done it, but with Mrs. Smith there was some sort of restraint that held her reply in check. Somehow, she sensed the elderly lady was not really prying just trying to show an interest in her, and it helped stave off her anger. Gradually, she simmered down, slowed her pace, and got hold of her senses.

CHAPTER

15

Chilled to the Bone

There was little traffic downtown in spite of the Christmas season. The streets and sidewalks were nearly deserted. The air was clear and cold, which, Loren decided, probably accounted for the lack of folks about town.

She tried to remember what Ted had told her yesterday about finding Lil Smith's. In her mind she reversed those directions, but before she had it all together correctly, she had walked two blocks in the wrong direction. By the time she had retraced the two blocks, she was ready for a good warming up. The air was unusually cold, but she kept on walking. Doctor Olsen's office was only a short distance beyond Town Hall, so she could warm up there. He probably wouldn't be back for a week or so, but since he seemed to be the only doctor in town, his nurse would likely be on hand to take his calls.

By the time she could see the sign, she was shivering

uncontrollably. Her disappointment when she reached the locked office was superseded only by the chill that gripped her. She stood for a minute in front of the office and looked at the padlock on the door. She'd have to go to Town Hall to get warm.

By the time she got hold of the big, old brass knob, her hand felt frozen. She could scarcely turn it.

Ted, inside, came to the rescue. "Loren, you're blue with cold! Come on in by the fire! Why, you shouldn't be out in this! It's much too cold for walking. I nearly froze walking over from my house, and you've come just as far if you've come from Lil Smith's."

He pulled off her mittens as he talked and massaged her stiff fingers. She tried to smile at him but her lips were rigid with cold.

"You need to get used to our weather," he scolded. "It's not like New Brunswick where the damp, cold air penetrates and you know you're getting too cold. Our cold is dry, and you can freeze a limb without even knowing it."

"How would you know about New Brunswick?" she asked through frozen lips.

"Why, I go there occasionally on business. Was there not too long ago, in fact, and let me tell you, their cold is painful! There's so much moisture in the air."

He pushed her into an overstuffed chair as he tried to get the blood flowing in her hands again, and now Loren began to feel slightly embarrassed by his attentiveness. "Hey! Leave me alone, Ted. I'm OK now. I'll recover!"

"You sure?"

"I'm sure!"

"Well, I'm walking home with you when you're ready

to go. You could freeze along the way. No one goes out around here on a day like this, especially for a walk."

"I can't let you walk home with me, Ted. It's too far for you to walk back again."

He smiled. "I won't walk back. Friend Bob has a car, remember? Hey! What were you doing out walking today anyhow?"

"I came to see if I could make an appointment with Doctor Olsen."

"Hey! That's too bad, isn't it?"

"What's too bad?"

"About Doc Olsen, I mean."

"What about Doc Olsen?"

"You haven't heard?"

She shook her head.

"They've taken him to a provincial center to see if they can straighten him out. The shock of that fire yesterday was too much, especially with everything else."

Loren began to feel impatient. He was assuming that she had always been part of this neighborhood. "Would you mind explaining all this?" she asked in bewilderment.

"Loren, I'm sorry. I just wasn't thinking about your not having met Doc Olsen until yesterday. Well, he lost his wife two months ago and almost had a nervous collapse. Then yesterday, everything that he had left of her went when he lost his home. All up in smoke! He has no children—no family to turn to for comfort—so it was just too much for him, I guess. He suffered amnesia. He couldn't even recall his own name, so they took him to the provincial for treatment. Too bad, too! Doc has a great mind."

"Is he the only doctor in town?"

"The only resident doctor. We have one who visits once a week from the next town, but Doc Olsen—why, he's a family fixture! Everybody loves Doc Olsen."

"I wonder when he'll be back."

"That's hard—practically impossible—to say."

Ted took note of her crestfallen expression and asked, "Did you have to see the doctor?"

"I've got to find out about Betty Schmitt."

"Oh, that. I'd almost forgotten about that. I thought you might not be well. As for Betty Schmitt—you can always ask Miss Claire."

"I'll not ask Miss Claire!"

"OK, sorry."

"I intend to wait for Doctor Olsen's return."

"You never can tell. You might have a long wait."

"Then there must be someone else in this crummy town that can help me out!" She spoke with such vehemence that he couldn't contain his look of surprise.

CHAPTER

16

Two Weeks Till Christmas

They trudged home unhurriedly. It wasn't quite as cold as it had been earlier in the day. To all appearances, Loren decided, Ted must be his own boss, for he closed up early without an explanation to anyone.

"Aren't you afraid someone will need something at Town Hall right after you leave?"

"Nah! Nothing goes on here in winter. A few marriages, but then I know about them and get certificates and forms out in plenty of time. The only thing I can't predict is a death. And you, my dear, are a complete surprise, for we never have visitors in winter. Since I took over the office three years ago you are the first winter visitor who has come looking for information."

"I'd have gone to China if I thought I might have turned up something about this Elizabett Schmitt."

"Boy! Do you sound desperate! You say she's a relative of yours?"

"My grandmother."

"Well, I suppose. . .if you never met her. . .it could be an obsession."

"It isn't just that!" Her voice was small and far off.

"Want to talk about it?"

She shook her head. "I'd rather not."

"Then let's talk about us. How'd you like the service last night?"

"It was all right, I guess."

"You guess! Don't you know?"

"Ted, I don't know you all that well, but this is one topic I'd rather not discuss."

"Why not?"

"Well, if you must know, I'm not a religious person! Never have been and have no intentions to be. OK?"

"Sure! Fine with me! I'm not a religious person myself."

She stared at him hard, not believing him. "You're teasing me."

"No. I mean it."

"Then. . .what. . ."

"I know, you're thinking about last night. What right do I have to talk like I did last night if I'm not religious?"

She nodded slowly in reply.

"OK, I'll tell you. Religion is often only a whitewash job, you know. A person calls himself a Christian. . .joins the church. . .that sort of thing, but nothing changes down inside. Deep in his heart, he's the same old person. But, take what happened to me. I didn't get religion, but I did give myself to the Lord. Loren, let me tell you, He changed me—inside out. He did a total overhaul on me. I became a new person. Oh, maybe everyone else thought

I got religion, but what I really got was the beautiful gift of salvation. A change of heart." He looked down at her and spoke softly. "He can do it for you, too."

"Ted, nothing can change this person. Furthermore, I don't desire to change. I want to be me. . .except that I wish I knew more about me," she added softly.

"God knows all about you!"

"I need to know. I just can't accept that God knows. I am here on a search. . .a quest. . . ."

"Well, I hope you find God in this quest of yours."

"I doubt it!" The answer was curt. Ted pressed her no further, and they walked to the house in silence.

Lil Smith invited Ted to stay for supper, and they spent an enjoyable evening over a Scrabble game. If it wasn't for Bob, Loren thought, I could almost let myself fall for this guy. There was something about Bob that infatuated her.

Tomorrow, she decided, she would get out the telephone number of her boss and call home. She wasn't sure what she should tell him, for she couldn't be certain when she could talk to Doctor Olsen. The way things were now, she decided, she would ask for a three-month extension. That meant she would try and get back to work by Easter.

Easter! What a dreadful thought—that she must plan ahead to Easter when it was now two weeks till Christmas.

Loren, deep in thought, lost interest in the Scrabble game, so Ted suggested they go for a walk. He made her bundle up well, although the temperature had risen some since the afternoon.

The night was beautiful. Snowflakes winked coquettishly back at the full moon.

"We're in for a storm," Ted pointed out. "Do you see that fuzzy halo around the moon? That's indicative of a storm of some kind within the next few days."

"I hope it's not too bad. There's already plenty of snow on the ground."

"Well, actually, snow would be much more welcome than rain. I like to see snow when the Christmas decorations are up. Just look back at the town from this hill. Aren't the lights beautiful?"

"I felt Christmasy in spite of myself when I walked downtown today. Then I got so cold I didn't feel much of anything." They laughed together.

"Christmas is a beautiful season, a result of God's gift to man."

Loren wasn't anxious to get into the religious aspects of Christmas. "This year, I'd just as soon see Christmas go by without being made aware of it."

"You don't like Christmas?" He looked at her, surprised.

"Oh, it's not that exactly. I like the decorations and all that's pretty about it, but without Dad. . .I wish it wouldn't come this year. . .There's an emptiness about it."

He put his arm about her shoulders and gave a gentle squeeze. "I'm sorry about your dad, Loren. It does make it hard to get through the Christmas season without your family, but you really don't have to feel empty, you know."

Uh, oh, she thought, I know where this is leading. "Let's forget it and go back, Ted. I've already been chilled once today."

"Boy! Am I inconsiderate. You sure didn't need more exposure to the cold."

"Oh, it's all right! I'm not really that cold."

They walked the rest of the way home in silence. By the time they stood on the Smith's doorstep, the moon had disappeared behind a cloud. It looked as if Ted's predictions of a storm were indeed going to materialize.

CHAPTER

17

Disappointing Discovery

January arrived. Loren got out her checkbook and examined the balance. She hoped she could make ends meet over Easter, but she was quickly using up her resources. How long had it been? Seven weeks? And the doctor had still not returned.

In desperation, she asked several individuals she met downtown if they knew Betty Schmitt, but no one recalled hearing the name. She even stopped Bob one day as he was coming out of the post office and put the question to him.

"No. I can't say I have, but you know, I used to know a chap by the name of Schmitt, a mechanic, in the neighboring town of Rivers He used to work on my car some. A real nice fellow."

"How far is Rivers?"

"Not far at all. Why?"

"I'd like to go there sometime."

"Anytime you want to go, just let me know. I have occasion to go over there once in a while myself. Actually, my fiancee, Beth, lives there." He smiled sheepishly.

"Oh, really?" Loren was taken aback, but she tried to sound enthusiastic. On Sunday night, she had almost gone to church with Bob. Now, she was glad she hadn't. She really didn't want to expose herself to the churchgoers' persuasiveness. She just couldn't accept the idea of a personal relationship with God. Surely God didn't care about her!

On Tuesday morning Bob didn't go to the church but informed Loren that he was going to Rivers. She wasted no time in getting ready, then had Bob take her directly to the garage where the man had worked. Loren was quivering with anticipation when she questioned the owner.

"You had a Schmitt work here?"

"Schmitt...Smith...whatever; they called him both. Yes, he was here for a period of three or four years."

"Can you tell me where he went when he left here?"

"No. I really can't say where he is, except that he went back home to British Columbia. His family's there. Sorry. I really can't help. He left no forwarding address."

Dead ends! That's all she ever reached! She just had to talk to Doctor Olsen. She wondered how he was progressing. She asked Bob if he knew when the doctor would return.

"No, I'm afraid I don't, but they tell me there's no change. It could be a year or more before he comes to grips with things, then again, it could happen overnight. Can't tell much about amnesia."

Before starting back, Bob stopped at an office building

Disappointing Discovery

downtown to see his girlfriend. "Would you like to come in and meet my fiancee?"

"Some other time, perhaps. I can't seem to keep my mind composed today. I think I might just look around the stores. This town is new to me."

With the knowledge she had acquired—first Bob's news of a fiancee, then the news on Doc Olsen—her brain seemed to stumble along, weaving in and out of orbit. The hopelessness of her situation left her totally discouraged. She might just as well go back east.

She was still feeling depressed when Ted came around after supper for one of their customary walks. "Something bothering you, Loren?"

"Oh, I'm just feeling down in the dumps, I guess."

"I wish you'd give the Lord a chance in your life."

"Ted, you're a religious nut! If you're going to get on that subject, I'm going back to the house."

"No! I promise not to talk about it, but that doesn't mean I can't pray."

She told him about her futile trip to Rivers. "If the doctor does not come home in two weeks time, I'm going back to New Brunswick."

"You're being ridiculously proud, Loren. You could go to Miss Claire."

"Never!"

She wanted to tell him about her disillusionment with Bob. She was sure he'd understand—but then, he might not. She was also quite sure that Ted himself was fond of her, but he made every effort to be no more than a friend. He had also made it clear at one point that he could never declare his love for a girl who didn't feel as he did about the Lord. She was sure that, for her, such a thing could never be. Oh, she liked Ted. But she couldn't accept his religion. Even for Bob, she couldn't have changed. He was just too old-fashioned.

In the days of waiting for Doc Olsen, she found Ted taking over her thoughts more and more. She knew she mustn't let herself get too involved, for she'd soon be heading home.

Lil Smith had grown close to Loren in the few weeks she'd spent there. It was almost like having a mother again, she thought, and she wondered how she would make out alone once more in her apartment. Cathy and Hazel were anxiously awaiting her return. They had kept in touch, and she was anticipating seeing her friends.

If only she could get the information her heart was set on. How could she go back without making one final effort? Miss Claire would have the answers, according to Ted and Doc Olsen.

No! She couldn't imagine herself going back to Miss Claire for information. On the other hand, was she going to let her lack of courage stop her in her quest for family and a sense of identity? Courage! Was that what she lacked?

She fell asleep mulling over the word.

CHAPTER

18

Confronting Miss Claire

Loren made up her mind. There was only one thing to do. If she wanted to locate her grandmother she had no other choice.

As she stood at the threshold of Miss Claire's, her heartbeat quickened, and she was tempted to turn and run before Miss Claire answered the door. Could she go through with it? This was the ultimate blow to her pride. With great hesitancy she took a step forward and rapped again.

Miss Claire didn't try to hide her surprise as she answered the knock. "Well! Miss Neilsen! And what brings you here? Lil Smith's prayers too much for you?"

Loren swallowed. "May I come in?"

Without directly answering, Miss Claire swung the door wide in reply and moved aside for Loren to enter.

In the minute it took her to remove her overshoes, Loren was able to regain a sense of composure. She took

In Search Of Yesterday

the chair Miss Claire offered and blurted with great urgency, "Miss Claire. . .I'd like to ask you something."

"You may ask, but I might find it necessary to withhold an answer." Her look of triumph and her pointed sarcasm almost caused Loren to recant, but Loren pushed on.

"Do you know where I can find Betty Schmitt?"

Miss Claire simply stared, profound shock written on her face. It was replaced by a sudden light of comprehension, as if a light had illuminated the darkened facts. She spoke just above a whisper to herself, "So that's it! Neilsen! Neilsen!" Then she sat down heavily in a chair opposite Loren and began to spin a story.

"Miss Neilsen, I've something to tell you from long ago—the distant past. Now that I think I've pieced this puzzle together, you'd probably prefer not to hear it, but it does concern the question you've just asked.

"A number of years ago, obviously before your time, Elizabett Schmitt and I were friends, close friends. At that time, she was a delightful girl, young and full of fun. Many a party we've attended together. But how time changes things! Elizabett, or Betty (as I always called her) married young. Her chosen was a no-good character who had nothing to give her. She did most of the providing, but anyway, they had a little girl—an only child. And she was a beautiful child. In fact" —Miss Claire scrutinized Loren closely for a minute—"yes, she even had the pretty auburn hair, but there the resemblance ends."

"Well, to make a long story short, when this daughter was about four years old, her mother got religion—old time religion, as she liked to call it. It was a bad case of fanaticism as far as I was concerned. Anyway, Schmitt might have been no good, but he was no fool! He knew his wife's fun life was over. He left her for another woman.

"Meantime, the daughter grew into the town beauty, and at a young age, she too began to 'partake of worldly pleasures' as her mother liked to call it. Actually, she was a fun-loving girl—just out to have fun, but some of the young men were out for their good times as well. At any rate, she went astray, and all Elizabett could do with this young'un was pray.

"Well, prayer didn't help, for daughter Elsie got more wild until one day she comes home with a baby son. She was just a kid herself, no more than fifteen, and...well, you'd think she'd straighten up, but she didn't. I guess she was just too much like her father. By the way, he had died in the meantime without ever getting in touch with his daughter. I wouldn't be surprised if that was where a lot of her rebellion came from, not having a dad. He didn't live that far away either, just over in the next town."

Loren was becoming impatient with the details, but she supposed the only way to get the story was to let Miss Claire tell it her way, so she made a special effort to sit back and relax.

"Anyway, to get back to Elsie—she switched boyfriends, and the second was worse than the first. His dad had originally come from eastern Canada, but they moved out here after he was born. He used to play the fiddle for all the dances around—a good-lookin' chap too. In fact, I can see his looks in you. You look like your father all right!"

Loren could feel the blood rushing to her face. Her anger was making her physically ill. This old gossip! This idle, old, tale bearing woman, sitting here in a state of bliss, telling her what she thought Loren didn't know!

Loren rose to her feet.

"Wait! I'm not finished! A year later, she had you and. . . ."

Loren snatched up her overshoes, and without putting them on, was out the door, while Miss Claire called after her, "Wait! Let me tell you where Betty is!" But her words trailed away on the wind. Loren was running now. Tears streamed down her face. Her feet were wet and cold, but she paid no heed. She just kept running, her overshoes swinging wildly at her side.

The church was right ahead. She could find quiet there. She pushed the door open without thinking it should have been locked. Dropping her overshoes in the vestibule, she went straight forward, literally throwing herself on the altar. Her body shook with heart-rending sobs, which echoed in the emptiness around her.

Loren lay there, face down on the sodden carpet, and came to a conclusion. She would go back to New Brunswick tomorrow if she could get a flight out on such short notice.

As thoughts of her failure to find her family tormented her mind, she was not aware of any conscious prayer, but something from her innermost being cried out, "Oh, God. . .if there is a God in heaven. . .why am I so abandoned? Why would You allow that old woman to gloat over my predicament? God, where are You? Why this sorrow. . .this emptiness? Doesn't anyone care?"

A hand touched her shoulder and she jumped in alarm.

"Sorry, I didn't mean to frighten you, but Loren, I know Someone who cares."

She looked around into Bob's face, and he explained. "I was in the office. I didn't mean to intrude, but believe me, I know Someone who cares for you a whole lot."

"Oh, Bob, you don't understand! And if you mean Ted cares for me, I know all about that, but I can't let Ted keep me here."

He interrupted. "I don't mean Ted!"

"Then who?"

"Loren, God cares! He really does! One reason why you are so unhappy is because you're resisting God. He loves you, and He wants you to love Him in return. I really mean it when I say He can bring you peace and joy."

"I. . .I can't love God! I hate that woman, and He'll expect me to get rid of my hate. But I can't. . .I hate. . .I simply hate her!"

"Who, Loren?"

"Why, that Miss Claire! I just came from there. She's the most awful, despicable, hateful old gossip I've ever seen!"

"God can take your hate if you'll give it to Him, Loren."

She looked at him, wanting to think he meant it, but not really believing.

"In fact," he added, "why don't you give Him yourself? That's all He asks, and He'll look after the rest. I promise you. It will change your life. He will change your life!"

"Will it give me what your mother has? Can God do that for me?"

"He sure can! As far as the hate, He can and will replace it with love, if you'll let Him. He wants to fill you with His Holy Spirit and make you over entirely—a new being—with joy like you've never known. All you need to do is come thirsting and hungering after God, and He'll fill you with Himself."

Slowly, timidly, wanting to believe what Bob had said, Loren dropped her head into her hands and began to pray falteringly.

"O God...You know all about my...my unhappiness...my unrest...and my...my need to belong. And Lord, You know how I hate Miss Claire...because... because of what she said about my wayward mother. And Lord, better than anyone else You know all about my painful past and the burden I bear because of it.

"O Lord, please...would You please take it all, and if You can, will You heal my wounded spirit and fill me with Yours." She lifted her face heavenward, tears streaming down her cheeks and dripping off her chin, as she continued, "O Father, please take my hurt and forgive me of my stubborn waywardness, and Lord, I want to thank You for dying for me—for taking my place and suffering for my sins. I don't really understand what's happening, but I do thank You for the great love I feel. Oh, thank You, Lord! Thank You!"

Bob watched with a great sense of elation as God began to do a work in her life. Suddenly, amid her tears, she began to laugh and rejoice in the Spirit, receiving what the Lord had for her. She finally submitted totally and let the Lord fill her with His Spirit and meet her need.

She turned a glowing countenance to Bob. "Oh Bob! It's wonderful! More than wonderful!"

"The joy of the Lord," Bob said softly, "You'll find it surpasses all your problems, Loren. Troubles have a way of getting smaller—fading into the background—

when we give the Lord our lives."

"Oh, Bob, I can't wait to get home and tell your mother!"

"And then we need to arrange for you to be baptized as soon as possible." He proceeded to explain about water baptism as they headed toward the car, with Loren listening intently and assenting eagerly.

Once in the car, Bob reached inside the glove compartment and pulled out a New Testament, which he held out to Loren. "I want you to have this. Read it every day, no matter where you are. You'll find the strength you need in these pages."

CHAPTER

19

A Step in the Right Direction

"Strange!" Bob said as he turned the doorknob at home. "It's locked. Mother never reminded me to take my key or said anything about going out this morning. In fact, she planned to stay home and welcome some guests from Oakville. They're coming for a couple of weeks of skiing, I believe."

He walked around to the front door, but it was locked, too. The next-door neighbor spotted him and stuck her head out the door. "Yahoo...Bob! Looking for your mother?"

"Did she go out?"

"Be right with you," she called and hurried inside for her coat.

As she came toward them Bob sensed an uneasiness. Something was wrong!

"Sorry, Bob. I wasn't sure where to contact you, and I planned to be right here when you arrived, but I had some baking in the oven. Had to check on that, and wouldn't you know, that's the time you'd come..."

He interrupted. "Where's Mother?"

"Well...Something happened this morning. She was hanging a few dish towels on the line there when I saw her stagger. Knew something was wrong..."

Bob's voice was urgent. "Tell me, is she all right? Where is she?"

"She's in the hospital, Bob, and they haven't called yet. I gave them my number, too, and the ambulance driver said..." Her final words were lost to their ears. Bob had grabbed Loren's hand and was already pulling her toward the car.

"Come on, Loren. We've got to get to the Brandon Hospital...no time to waste. That woman prattles on and on. She means well, but in an emergency, you'd think she'd realize."

Twenty minutes later they were at the emergency desk asking for Lil Smith. The nurse checked the records. "Well, she was brought in here about an hour ago. The doctor's with her at the present time."

"Is she...is she all right?"

"Are you a relative?"

"Her son...Please..." Bob's voice was rising impatiently.

"Just have a seat. I'll check with the doctor." And the nurse was swishing her way down the hall.

She returned, after what seemed an eternity to Bob, and beckoned them to follow as she led the way to the intensive care unit.

A Step in the Right Direction

"Oh, no," Bob groaned, "this must be bad!"

Outside a closed door, the nurse stopped and indicated a couple of chairs nearby.

"You can wait there. The doctor will be with you in a minute."

"But is she...alive?"

"Well, of course! But sick, nonetheless. Dr. Baye will explain it to you." And she was gone once more.

Bob slumped into one of the chairs, his head in his hands. There was no sound for several moments, only his impatient sighs and whispered prayers. Suddenly the reality of what had happened hit Loren. Obviously the woman was in serious condition to be in the intensive care unit, perhaps beyond medical help, and she had not yet asked the question which had so long occupied her thoughts.

Now she realized she had been waiting for courage, hoping that sometime she would find the boldness to ask Lil Smith if she had ever known a Betty Schmitt. After all, Miss Claire had obviously known her, and since she and Lil Smith had been best friends it was more than likely Lil had known her, too. Now it might be too late.

She should have asked before, but she could not be sure what Lil's reaction would be. She seemed to be such a pious woman. What if she guessed the connection between Loren and the promiscuous Elsie, Elizabett's daughter? No, Loren had never had the courage to enquire.

The door opened quietly, and a nurse moved noiselessly away from them. A doctor moved through the open doorway, pulling off his stethoscope as he came towards them. Glancing only briefly in Loren's direction, he turned

In Search Of Yesterday

to Bob. "Mr. Smith?"

Bob nodded and got slowly to his feet.

"I'm Doctor Baye." He stuck out his hand in acknowledgement, and Bob clasped it firmly. The doctor hurried on, "Your mother's a very sick woman. She has suffered a cardiac arrest and is presently unconscious."

"Oh, Lord!" Bob's groan was a mere whisper.

"Right now she's doing OK, but she needs around-the-clock care."

"Can I see her?" Bob broke in quickly.

"There's really not much point—she can't talk to you."

"But please, just for a minute. I must see her. . .to know she's. . .all right."

"For your reassurance and peace of mind, you may see her briefly." The doctor nodded toward the door from which he had just emerged and Bob, with an "I won't be long," entered. Loren rose hesitantly and started to follow Bob into the room, when the doctor stopped her with a question. "Are you her daughter or related in some way?"

"No."

Dr. Baye laid a restraining hand on her arm. "Sorry, no admittance."

"But. . ."

"Immediate family only, and then one at a time. You should read the sign on the door," he said firmly and then stepped back into the room behind Bob.

CHAPTER 20

Chilling News

"Spare her, Lord," Loren prayed. "I want to tell her what's happened to me. Don't let it be too late—she'd be so happy, I know, if she could only understand what's been taking place in my life."

The door opened and Bob came out. True to his word, he had not overstayed his time. It had been no more than two minutes. Loren looked at him questioningly. His eyes were full of pain, his jawline taut, as he struggled to keep his composure.

"Oh, Loren. She looks awful! Simply awful! She's as gray as death...the most terrible color...and so still...with all those tubes attached."

Loren patted his arm comfortingly, recalling her own father's death just weeks ago. There was nothing she could say. What did a person say at a time like this? She could not recall a single thing anyone had said to her. Her grief had been too intense.

Bob paced back and forth across the waiting room. There seemed to be no one else around, and if there had been, he would have been oblivious to the fact.

Finally Loren asked, "Should we wait here, Bob? Just what should a person do?"

He looked at her, his stupor receding. "Sorry, Loren. I guess I forgot you were actually here. Let me go talk to the doctor again, and if everything's safe, I could drive you home. I can come back later." Aside, he uttered half aloud, "O Lord, don't let anything happen while we're gone."

Loren shook her head vigorously. "You're not going home just to take me! I'm waiting here with you. I'd never forgive myself if something should. . .happen. . .after we left."

"But. . .you're not related. You don't need to wait. It would be different if you were family. It's inconsiderate of me to keep you here. Let me go call Beth. She'll come in. She would certainly want to know anyway. I should have thought to call her before this."

Loren's voice took on an authority she didn't know she possessed. "Call Beth if you like, but I'm staying. And as far as family—this is the closest I've come to being family anywhere. . .back in the land of my roots. Your mother has made me feel so much at home. . .almost like a daughter."

She stopped, her eyes welling with tears. Bob laid a gentle hand on her shoulder, and suddenly she was crying against his chest, sniffling and trying to control her sobs while Bob gently patted her back.

"What am I doing?" She stepped back, brushing away the teardrops. "Here you are, needing someone to stand by you—help you through this—and I go blubbering all over the place. You'd better call Beth. She'd likely be more of a help. Anyway, she needs to know."

Bob nodded and left to find a telephone.

Loren sat back down and tried to get a grip on herself. Mrs. Smith had become more like a mother than anything else, and strangely enough, Loren didn't feel like a lodger. The Smiths made her feel so much at home. She should have kept aloof—kept herself at a distance—and never allowed herself to become so much a part of this family. She knew better than to get so involved with strangers, but then they had never seemed like strangers. When she found her grandmother it was going to be difficult to say farewell to these folks.

A nurse came out of the room and approached her. "Mrs. Smith's daughter, I presume?"

"No. Just a friend."

"Is her son still here?"

"He's gone off to find a phone somewhere."

The nurse wheeled about and quickly hurried away.

"Well," Loren spoke to the empty room, "what was that all about? Could something have happened to Lil Smith?"

There was an urgency about the nurse's behaviour. Something had happened. Loren was almost sure of it. For the second time that day, she prayed, "O Lord, please spare her. I want her to know."

CHAPTER

21

Life and Death Situation

"Loren, Beth's coming in to stay awhile, and I'm taking you home."

For a minute, Loren was reluctant to agree and about to raise her voice in protest, then thought better of it. It seemed only natural that Bob would prefer having his fiancee here with him. "Bob, I really don't mind staying, and I hate for you to have to drive me clear back to Neuberg."

"It's all right. I just talked to the doctor, and he says there's nothing anyone can do. Time alone will tell the tale. The next forty-eight hours are critical, but at present nothing has changed, and only family members can see her anyhow. You might as well be home. There really is no point in your staying. Go home and fix yourself something to eat. At least, you will be able to relax a bit. I'll be home as soon as there is something definite. I just can't leave her as long as I don't have any answers. You do understand, don't you?"

She nodded her head, not daring to express how she felt. The Smiths were the nearest thing to a family she had, yet she knew she couldn't claim the right to relationship. Poor Lil! Tears blurred her eyes as she followed Bob out to the parking lot. After all, it was only chance that had brought her to this place—or was it? Reluctantly, she climbed into the car beside Bob.

"When you get home," he said, "check to see if there's any word from that family from Oakville, will you? Maybe there'll be a note or something tucked under the door. Or perhaps they've left some word with Mrs. Anderson next door—the lady who told us. I suppose it would be best if I went to check with her. She probably has the key anyway, though she never mentioned it this morning. But then, I guess I never really gave her a chance. Since you need to get in, I'll go over there and see."

Bob's voice had trailed off until Loren felt that he was merely talking to himself. The remainder of the journey transpired in silence.

It turned out that Mrs. Anderson was away when they arrived home.

"No neighbor—no key," Bob reported. "Now what do we do?"

"Are there no other guests who might have a key?"

Bob shook his head. "No one. We need two rooms for this family of four, and Mr. Spear's room was turned over to you. As you know, the family from Oakville couldn't possibly have a key yet. Mother was waiting for them to arrive." Bob frowned thoughtfully. "I suppose there is one solution. I could take you to Miss Claire's."

For a minute, she thought he must be joking, but

Life and Death Situation

when she realized the predicament they were in, she knew he was being serious.

"It would only be for tonight," he added quickly. "I'm sure Mrs. Anderson will be back by tomorrow, or Mother will be able to give us an answer; something will turn up by then. Think you can stand it for one night?"

Her nod of consent was a surprise even to herself.

"I'll call you just as soon as there is some word on Mother's condition and let you know how things are."

Bob's words of reassurance as he left her at Miss Claire's door were almost lost in the malevolent stare of the latter. Loren was no longer so sure she should have consented to come, although one thing she did know: she no longer hated Miss Claire. Somehow she felt a sense of shame and sorrow for this ill-mannered woman, who apparently thrived on other people's troubles. How dreadful to be so enslaved with such a personality disorder.

Loren's thoughts sped into oblivion at Miss Claire's obnoxious greeting. "Well, well. If it isn't little Miss Runaway! I suppose your curiosity got the best of you, and you've come back for the rest of the information?"

"No! I need a place for the night."

"Well, I do have plenty of room. Have always had more and better facilities than Lil Smith. Never could understand why people went to that 'religious institution' to stay. Well, come in and tell me what's happened to Lil. Where were you when it happened? Off gallivantin' I suppose. And that offspring, Bob—why wasn't he home with her?"

Her questions tumbled over each other in her haste to get all the news, although she didn't once inquire about the state of her former friend's health. Patiently Loren begin her explanation of Bob's absence, but Miss Claire stopped her almost at once.

"You don't have to explain his absence to me. I know all about him. Leaves his aged mother and goes down to that church office day after day. It's all her own fault. She brought him up that way. I guess she deserves what she gets. It's just too bad he didn't have some common sense! Why, Lil Smith's getting to be an old lady. She's no spring chicken, that's for sure!"

Loren almost bit her tongue to keep from reminding her that she and Lil Smith had once been girlhood friends. Instead of offering further comment, she took the key Miss Claire proffered and went straight to her room.

The evening loomed ahead ominously, but she occupied herself with prayer for Miss Claire, Lil Smith and Bob. Finally, she wound up her evening with letters to Hazel and Cathy. She hated to relate her dead-end situation to Cathy, but then, that's what friends are for.

CHAPTER

22

Back at Miss Claire's

Loren could hardly believe she was back at Miss Claire's as she opened her eyes in response to the morning sunlight flooding her room. But then her new-found sense of joy welled up, and peace flooded her being. What a bright morning the Creator had given—a beautiful new day without guilt! It was great to be alive. Even being at Miss Claire's couldn't dampen her enthusiasm or obliterate the joy she felt. But what of Lil? Bob hadn't called yet, as he had said he would, so apparently she was still alive.

Well, no time to linger in bed. She glanced at her watch. It was already 7:20. "My goodness!" she exclaimed, then quickly donned her robe and lunged for the bathroom, only to meet Miss Claire's disapproving glare in the hall.

"Well! I wondered if you were going to get up today. Not sick are you?" She eyed her suspiciously. "You said you had been to see Doc Olsen."

Loren could feel her face flaming and for a moment had to clench her jaw to subdue the retort instigated by her rising anger. Silently she sent up a prayer: "Lord, help me!" Then she smiled in spite of her embarrassment and went into the bathroom.

There she let the tears flow down her cheeks unchecked. How could that woman make such insinuations! She was so callous! Loren wondered what she should have done. Should she have retorted as was her previous manner? Should she have tried to make some mild comment? No, she had done the right thing. She could think of no response that would have been appropriate. The woman lacked good manners and obviously knew nothing about the milk of human kindness.

Loren decided to skip breakfast. Miss Claire served the first meal of the day at 7:30. She was already late, and there was nothing to be gained by another confrontation. If Bob didn't call shortly, she would ring the hospital and see how Lil was.

Refreshed from her bath she went back to her room and reached in her purse for the New Testament Bob had given her. She recalled that shortly before her mother had died she had also given her one. It had been during that difficult period of rebellion in her teens, and Loren now wondered what she had done with it. It was probably still stuffed away in a packing box somewhere. She wondered why she hadn't turned to it for help when her father died, but then it wasn't the customary thing for her to do. She wasn't used to going to the Word of God for comfort, or any other reason for that matter.

Not knowing where to begin reading in the New

Back at Miss Claire's

Testament, she simply thumbed through it, letting it fall open at will. Some passages she was not sure she understood, while others seemed to jump out at her, lifting her spirits and increasing her faith. She became so engrossed that she didn't even hear Miss Claire call her to the telephone. When she knocked at the door, Loren jumped nervously and called, "Come in!"

"Well. .ll. . . ! I see Lil Smith has a convert!" She paused, then said shortly, "Telephone for you."

Loren slipped quickly past her with a nod of thanks and hoped that Miss Claire would not follow her to the phone. She turned her back to the stairs and spoke as softly as possible. It was Bob, as she had hoped, but he hastily told her there was nothing new to report. There had been no change. Lil was still unconscious and still listed as critical. Only time and prayer would tell the tale.

"Did you find out any more about the guests, Bob? You know, I could go back to the house and do what has to be done for them in your mother's absence. I'd be more than happy. . ."

"No need," he interrupted, "I got hold of Mrs. Anderson just minutes ago. She was there when they arrived yesterday and sent them on their way. Well, actually, she sent them to. . .Hey! Aren't they there?"

"What do you mean. . .here?"

"She said she sent them to Miss Claire's until things got settled here. She wasn't sure of Mother's condition. They must still be there. . .unless they drove clear back to Oakville."

"They could be here, Bob. I really don't know. I do know there are some others here. They're at breakfast at the moment, but I just haven't mingled yet. I guess. . .I didn't feel like it last night, and this morning, well...I didn't have the courage to...to face Miss Claire. I was a few minutes late getting up, and she's very touchy about that sort of thing...so..."

"Well, look, I have to run, Loren, but if the guests are there and indicate they want to leave, maybe you could mention the alternative you suggested. I really don't want to put an extra load on you, but then again, I'd hate to see their two-week vacation plans spoiled. On the other hand, if they are content to stay there..."

"But Bob! What about me? I'm not content to stay here, and I plan to go at once to Mrs. Anderson's for the key!" Loren struggled valiantly to keep the tremor out of her voice.

"Sorry, Loren! I know it's difficult for you, and if you wish to go back to the house, that's fine, but the guests...well, unless they indicate they wish to move out of Miss Claire's...you know how it is. And you couldn't very well plan to stay at the house while I'm there alone."

Loren could feel a flush creep into her cheeks as she mumbled a response. Of course, Bob was right. It might be all right for her to go to the house now while Bob was still at the hospital, but to stay overnight? It would never do for Miss Claire to get wind of this predicament. Somehow, the guests had to be persuaded to come back to Mrs. Smith's.

CHAPTER 23

Alternate Arrangements

Loren was relieved when Bob hung up with the promise to call again in the next twenty-four hour period with another report. Reluctantly, she turned to go back upstairs. She could smell fresh coffee and sizzling bacon, and for just a moment she hesitated indecisively.

"Well, there's plenty of breakfast left, Miss Neilsen, if you'd like a bite, even though you are late."

Although Loren had not heard her hostess approach, Miss Claire was standing partway down the stairs with what Loren would later describe to Bob as a half smile, half smirk on her face.

"It's. . .it's all right. I'm really not terribly hungry."

She looked at Miss Claire again, sensing that she had probably been there during the entire conversation. Her gaze faltered under the older woman's scrutiny. She decided that rather than to pass her on the steps, perhaps it would be better to join the other guests for breakfast.

"Well...maybe...just some coffee," she said hesitantly and made her way into the dining room. At a glance she noticed seven other guests were present. Apparently they had been introduced to each other already, as conversation was flowing garrulously. Everyone seemed to be participating except for the permanent residents, Mr. Hayes and Miss Barnes. The latter simply looked bored, nodded at Loren as she sat down and passed a few polite remarks about the weather.

Miss Claire busied herself pouring coffee and suddenly startled Loren by speaking at her elbow as she poured. Loren even thought she detected a note of real concern in her voice.

"Anything new on Lil Smith?"

"Nothing at the present."

"Well, you know I couldn't help but overhear; then again, I did know it was Bob's voice. I believe my guests were one of the topics discussed."

Embarrassed, Loren was lost for words. What could she say? Were those same guests present at breakfast? As if in answer to her unspoken questions, Miss Claire continued, "Miss Neilsen, this is Mr. and Mrs. Howe and their sons from Oakville." She nodded toward a couple seated toward the other end of the long dining room table. At either side sat a teen-ager looking slightly uncomfortable and out of place amid the adults.

The Howes attempted a pleasant response, and Mrs. Howe introduced the boys, Marty and Matt, their fifteen year-old twins, more fully. "I'm afraid the boys are rather glum about the way things have turned out. We had planned to stay at the Smith residence, and our itinerary was fully laid out for the two-week period. Due to the illness, our plans have to be changed. We don't even know what was planned for today. By the time things get straightened out, a good part of this week will probably be gone—hence the boys' state of gloom."

Loren smiled in their direction, but they quickly averted their gaze. "Perhaps I could get hold of the itinerary for you." Loren watched the boys' faces take on a new interest. Matt even went so far as to return her smile this time. "I've been staying at Mrs. Smith's myself. Her son, Bob, looks after the planning so he. . ."

"Oh, could you really find out for us?" Mrs. Howe was beaming at the boys. "It would be so much more convenient if we knew something definite. . . .I mean, our plans have been made for three months now, and to have them spoiled like this. . ."

"I'll see what can be done."

Loren excused herself and started for the telephone. On second thought she decided to get her coat. She could see Miss Claire's jaw jutted firmly out and an indefinable gleam in her eye. Anger perhaps?

At the door, she reached out to take Loren firmly by the arm. "Remember," she hissed, "I want no trouble. These are my guests at the present time, and believe it or not, I can make things unpleasant for you."

As if Loren didn't know! Without responding to the threat, she slipped past Miss Claire and out the door. She estimated the nearest telephone booth to be about four blocks away. During her first eventful stroll about town, she had seen a couple of them, side by side. Now she racked her brain to recall just where that had been. On the day of her long walk to Doc Olsen's office, she remembered passing Dawson's Pharmacy, and the telephones

In Search Of Yesterday

had not been too far from that. She quickened her pace. In contrast to that first walk, she found this one merely invigorating in the frosty morning air.

Suddenly Loren realized that, while deep in thought, she had just passed Dawson's Pharmacy. She retraced her steps. Sure enough, just beside the pharmacy were the booths. She let herself into the first one and fished in her purse for a dime. Finding the hospital number, she dropped her dime into the slot and dialed. Nothing happened. She tried again, then realized the telephone was out of order. She moved to the next one and redialed. This time it rang through, and she had the hospital operator page Bob Smith. Her mind was in a turmoil as she waited for him to take her call.

After what seemed like ages she heard his voice. "Hello!" When he realized it was Loren, his voice became edged with concern. "What's your problem? Anything serious?"

"Sorry to bother you, Bob," Loren apologized, "but those guests are at Miss Claire's, and they're wondering about some sort of itinerary. Do you know anything about it?"

"Oh, great! The itinerary's on the kitchen table at home, and I can't leave yet. Things could go either way!"

"Can I get it? I mean. . .would you mind if I went in to see what's scheduled for them?"

"Oh, today's no problem! At 2:00 p.m. Bob Bristow's bringing their skis out in the pickup, and he'll lead them back to Arrow Creek so they can take the ski trail back to town. They should be back by six o'clock, I would think. They're supposed to come back to a 'piping hot meal' according to the brochure, but with Miss Claire. . .well, I'm not sure she'll change her schedule to coincide with theirs. You know how she is. When it's her mealtime—that's it. It's officially mealtime."

"Oh, Bob! This isn't going to work. I can just feel it in my bones. I don't see why we can't carry on as planned. I could go out there and look after getting that meal. I'm going to tell them so, when I get back to Miss Claire's. I'm at a phone booth right now."

"I'm not so sure you should, Loren."

"But their plans are really fouled up this way. Why can't I go over there and bring them back with me? I promise. . .I can take care of them, and we can carry on as planned."

"Are you sure? You might have Miss Claire down your throat."

"I can manage. All that I dread is informing Miss Claire, but with my new-found strength, I will do it honestly."

"It would be a lot better for all concerned if you think you can handle it."

"Oh, I can."

"And Loren? Why not let them tell Miss Claire? And are you sure you want to go through with this? There's an awful lot of work involved, you know."

"Of course, I want to do it! For Lil's sake. And for mine, too. I'll be more than glad to help out any way I can."

The walk back to Miss Claire's seemed shorter until she got within sight of the house, then she began to wonder what she should say. Finally she stopped dragging her feet and chided herself, "Oh, for Pete's sake, they're our guests and not Miss Claire's anyway. Why, they signed on at Mrs. Smith's guest house, and that's where they're going. I will be in charge of them until Lil Smith's return. They're my responsibility." With that remark, she marched determinedly into the house.

CHAPTER

24

Filling the Gap

To Loren's delight, Miss Claire was tied up on the phone and seemed to be arguing intensely with a creditor. Loren took advantage of the situation to inform the Howes of her idea and invite them back to the original guest house of their plans. They were delighted that she had been able to recover their itinerary and went to collect their luggage.

As they came down the stairs with their bags, Loren could tell Miss Claire was not at all pleased. She cupped the mouthpiece in her hand, and Loren simply stated the situation. A tirade followed them out the door, but Loren walked out with a sense of relief. She had paid well for her one-night stay and, in addition, made sure she left a healthy tip. She felt certain her guests had done the same. Now she hastily fled out the front door, leaving the angry woman fuming to her telephone victim. She breathed a great sigh of relief when she realized that neither she nor the Howes were being pursued by Miss Claire.

"Wow!" Marty commented, "I bet she melted the telephone wire."

Mrs. Howe was the only one to hesitate. "Perhaps we shouldn't do this, dear. After all we were in a pinch, and she did take us in."

"What? You're not backing down are you? As you well know, she got her pay for what she did. We're only carrying out our original plans. Come on, or we're going without you."

They climbed into the car, forgetting for the moment that they had an extra passenger.

"Oh, right! Miss Neilsen! Uh. . .perhaps you could get in the back with the boys."

"I could walk over," she offered, "but then I guess you'd have to wait for me to get the key from the neighbor." Reluctantly, she got in between the twins. She was glad they hadn't far to go, for the twins seemed none too happy.

After getting the key from Mrs. Anderson, she went at once to check on the itinerary, hoping desperately that Bob had been right about where he left it. It was there! She scanned it briefly, then explained about Mr. Bristow's coming for them at two o'clock. She hadn't the vaguest notion where the ski trail might be and hoped they would not question her about it. The boys were quick to spot the record player, but to their disappointment, they could find nothing but gospel music and a few classics. They settled for a country gospel number, and the air soon resounded with its vibrations.

"Hey!" Matt complained, "that's not exactly music

Filling the Gap

to dance to. Don't you have any other records around here?"

"Sorry, but gospel music seems to be all that Mrs. Smith enjoys."

"What is she? A religious freak?" Marty wanted to know.

"I used to think so," Loren smiled, "but I've changed my mind. She's really quite a lady!"

"You her daughter or something?"

"Just a friend."

"No relation?"

"No. She gave me a place to stay when I had nowhere else to go—except Miss Claire's."

"Well, in my book, that would qualify her as a friend, all right. Did you hear what she said to my dad?"

"Yeah, and Marty, tell her what she said last night."

"Nah, that was just a lot of idle gossip. Dad said it wasn't worth the time he spent listening to her, but we were in the same boat you were—no place to go."

Loren came to Miss Claire's defense. "I really think she means well. I think it's just her way."

"Some way, I'd say!"

The boys wandered off as she prepared to fix lunch. What should she get? What had Lil planned? Was there a menu or a record somewhere? She checked cupboard drawers, but found nothing. Deciding to prepare whatever she could find, she reached into the cupboard for a pot to heat soup. There, taped on the inside of the cupboard door, was the menu for the week. "Thank you, Lord," she whispered. "That will make things so much easier this week, then, by next week. . ." Her thoughts that Lil might then be home trailed off. She was not even sure Lil was conscious yet.

Loren reached for the skillet to make hamburgers for the lunch. "Everyone like hamburgers?"

Her question drew an avid response from the teenagers. "Yeah, great!"

Marty added, "Make it two for me, please, and Matt'll want the same."

"Then two it'll be!"

The adults laughed good-naturedly, and to Loren's embarrassment, asked if she would show them to their rooms so they could get unpacked.

As Loren came back to the kitchen the telephone was ringing. It was Bob. "Hi, Loren. I wondered if you got in OK. Are the folks there?"

"Uh huh, and everything's fine. I even found your Mom's menu for the week. I must admit I was at the point of panic when I found it, though."

"Mother always tapes it inside a cupboard door. But listen, Loren. I've got some news. The doctor says Mom is going to be all right, but it will take some time for her to be her old self again. She regained consciousness, and I was in to see her for a minute. She looks so much better! They wouldn't let us converse, but she smiled encouragement and that helped. Thank the Lord! I just know she's going to be all right."

"Oh, Bob! I'm so glad! It's been pretty hard to get my mind on anything else, though I've kept fairly busy since I came back here. Did the doctor tell you what happened?"

"Yeah. It was a heart attack. He's keeping her for the remainder of this week, but things are really looking up. They're taking her out of intensive care in the morning, if she keeps showing improvement as she has been. I can see such a difference in her appearance."

"That's great! And thanks, Bob. Thanks for letting me know. I'm happy for your mother, but I'm glad for your sake, too. I knew you were terribly worried."

"I sure was! But I left it in God's hands. Now that she's conscious, I'm going to try to get back in to see her for a few minutes; then I think I'll go into the office this afternoon for awhile. That means I'll be home at the usual time. Is there anything you need, Loren?"

"Nothing but prayer." She laughed. "It looks like your Mom had things well organized here. . .and it's a good thing. I'll do what I can to hold things together until you get home."

"Good. I'll see you at five then."

Loren walked away from the telephone lighter of step and lighter of heart. She was almost certain she would get a chance to tell Lil Smith about the change the Lord had made in her life.

CHAPTER

25

Home at Last

The next two weeks went from one extreme to another. At times it seemed they dragged by, and then suddenly they would seem to leap away from her. She did her best to do what she felt was required—what Lil Smith might have done under the circumstances—but she was never quite sure she had done the right thing or in the way Lil Smith might have done it.

On some days, before she got through her morning chores, she would find herself gazing in amazement at the clock which told her it was time to prepare supper. Although she threw herself into the work with gusto, she still failed to accomplish some of the tasks she set for herself. But then she never had run a household for six people before. At times, she felt as though the last Saturday would never come and the guests would never leave, but suddenly it was their final Saturday, and she was rushing about stripping beds, cleaning guest rooms and doing a hundred other weekend housecleaning chores.

The Howes departed rather reluctantly, promising to return on their next major holiday. By that time, Loren mused, her search would probably be over, and she would either be at her grandmother's house or back in New Brunswick. She was getting more anxious than ever to reach the end of her quest. In the midst of her thoughts, the telephone rang.

"Hey, Loren! You can't guess what!" Bob's excitement carried over the wire.

"No, I can't," she laughed, "but it sounds good. Tell me about it."

"I'm bringing Mom home! The doctor released her this morning."

"What! When?"

"Right away—as soon as she's ready, and she's getting ready this minute. Isn't that great?"

"Well, I'll say! How is she feeling?"

"She says fine, and she looks good, but Dr. Baye says she's to rest quietly for another two weeks. She can make trips to the table and bathroom and that's the extent of it until he's seen her again, then he'll give her further instructions. But isn't it wonderful? We'll be home in a couple of hours. Just in time for supper! See you then." And he was gone.

Loren glanced at the clock in dismay. Well, she'd make things as presentable as possible in the next two hours. Fortunately she already had a stew simmering for supper. Now she needed to get the living room straightened up a bit and the dusting done.

By the time Bob helped his mother into the house, things were as neat as a pin. Tired from the journey, Lil

Home at Last

Smith lay on the sofa, and Loren brought her a cover. She smiled her thanks but made no effort to talk as Loren spread the meal on the table and helped her to her place, asking, "Would you like me to bring you a tray instead?"

"Oh, no! I'm too anxious to sit at my own dining room table again. I just needed that little rest after the trip home. I feel better now. And it's so good to be home!"

"It's good to have you home." Loren gave her frail shoulder a squeeze.

"I see Bob had a qualified housekeeper at work in my absence," Lil added, smiling at the two of them. "Now, Bob, if you'll just return thanks."

Bob could wait no longer to have Loren break the news of her experience, and as soon as thanks was returned, he broached the subject. "Mother, Loren has some good news!" He nodded at Loren.

"Oh, Mrs. Smith, I was so afraid when I heard how sick you were that I wouldn't get to tell you this!" Loren's eyes misted with tears.

"Well, don't keep me in suspense! Tell me, Loren, what is it? Something has happened," she said, as she looked at the tears sparkling in Loren's eyes.

Bob could contain it no longer. . .the news had to be broken. "Loren's given her heart to the Lord and received His Spirit. And all because of Miss Claire!"

A smile spread slowly across his mother's face.

"She wasn't really responsible," Loren laughed. "She just made me so mad I got to the end of myself. . . ."

"And you turned to God. Well, praise the Lord!" Lil Smith wiped at her own eyes. "Tell me all about it, child."

"There's not much more to tell. . .except that Miss Claire made me so mad, that I almost. . .well. . .I. . .

I. . .almost gave up my quest."

"Your quest?"

"Yes, my search. You see, I asked her a question about someone, and she went into all this detail about. . .well. . .about my illegitimacy and. . ." Loren stared at Lil Smith in alarm. "Hey, are you all right?"

Bob jumped up and went to his mother. Her face had turned a ghastly white, and when she spoke, her voice was so small that Loren almost missed the question. "Who. . .who did you ask about?"

"My grandmother. You know, I bet you'd know her, too. You must be close to Miss Claire's age, and you've lived here all your life. . .but Doc Olsen said I should ask Miss Claire."

"Who. . .who. . .?" Mrs. Smith gasped.

"Elizabett Schmitt."

For a moment, both Bob and Loren thought the older woman was going to collapse, then dabs of color broke out on her cheeks, and tears slowly streaked them. On wobbly legs, she rose slowly to her feet and reached out to Loren. "Oh, child! child! You've come home! I'm Betty Schmitt, your grandmother!"

When the realization struck Loren, she was in her grandmother's arms in one swoop.

Bob, tears on his own cheeks, merely stood and watched, offering a prayer of thanks for whatever was happening. All at once Lil Smith realized she was leaving him out. She welcomed him into the circle of her arms also. "Bob," she said, "come and meet your sister."

CHAPTER

26

Kin-Folks

The elation Loren felt was beyond anything she had hoped for or dreamed possible.

"Imagine," she said to Bob after supper, "finding the Lord and finding my family in such a short space of time."

Her grandmother smiled at her. "That's just like the Lord," she said. "I've been praying for my granddaughter for years. When I got word that Elsie had passed away, I felt like a part of me died, and I almost gave up hope. But not quite. Thank God, I kept on praying. Nothing's impossible with God!"

"How come you never told me about all this, Mother?" Bob sounded dejected—a little neglected even.

"What purpose would it have served? Maybe it would have only lowered your self-esteem. I decided there would come a time—God's time. And I'm glad I waited for it. As far as I was concerned, Bob, you were always my son. You were only a year old when Loren was born. Elsie left you with me at that time, so I adopted you. You've always known me as 'Mother.'

"When I was twenty-eight years old, Hans left me for another woman, so I decided I needed a new start. Most of my friends were already calling me Lil, not Betty, and then I Anglicized my German name from Schmitt to Smith. Most people have forgotten who Betty Schmitt is. They only know Lil Smith."

She paused and silence filled the room. "It wasn't easy trying to start again, but I turned this place into a guest house, and in a year or two, I was back on my feet. I had found the Lord a few years before that, so He was on my side. Just about the time Hans left, the Lord became so real to me. Hans hated religion in any form and was never happy to see me go to church. But with God's help I've survived it all, and this"—she reached out and put an arm around each of them—"is the culmination of my wildest dreams. I have only one regret. I lost my precious daughter. Loren, do you remember. . .did she ever pray?"

"I. . .I don't know. I was only twelve years old when she died. I know she did change when I began to mature. I'm afraid I was a bit hard to manage at times. Dad even threatened to send me back with you if I didn't straighten up." She stopped, her mind going back to the days following her mother's death.

Suddenly she reached over and patted Bob's hand, injecting a lighter note into the atmosphere. "I must say, I never knew I had a handsome brother somewhere."

"He looks just like your mother, Loren. Elsie was a very pretty girl. You're a combination of both your parents. Except for your hair, you tend to favor your father."

Loren chuckled. "I guess I dare say this now, Bob. I think I fell in love with you the first time I saw you. There was just something special about you. Now that I've heard about a future sister-in-law, I can honestly say it's just sisterly love. When you first told me about her, my first inclination was to get away from here. . .away from you. . .away from my hurt, but now I'm glad I stayed. Why, I've even learned to like Ted."

"Only like?"

"Well, maybe a brotherly love," she teased.

"But he's not your brother."

"No, Bob, let's just say seriously I'm not sure where I stand, but I do like him. . .a lot."

The doorbell rang.

"Come in!"

Ted stuck his head in the open doorway.

"Speak of the devil!"

"If you're eating, I won't bother you. I'll just take a minute. I came by to see if Loren would like to go for a walk." He looked in Loren's direction, then stepped in and closed the door, surprise masking his face at the sight of her. "Hey, Loren! What's happened to you? You look so different tonight."

"I'll tell you later," she teased, "while we walk. First I need to find the phone pad I laid down. I wrote my ex-boss's phone number on it, and I've got to call and tell him I won't be back at Easter as planned."

"Never mind your boss. Call him tomorrow. Come on, Loren. I want to know what happened."

Bob held up a pad of paper. "Is this what you were looking for, Loren?"

She nodded.

"Well, why couldn't I call this number and tell them you're not returning. I think Ted deserves an explanation of what's going on."

"Go ahead, Bob, and thanks! Tell him I've decided to stay home."

Bob winked at her. "It's as good as done! Now will you and Ted go for that invigorating walk?"

"Thanks! What a brother! My quest is over. Search complete. Ted, I'm so glad we bumped into each other."

He looked at her in bewilderment for a minute, then they both burst into gales of laughter. Taking Ted's hand, she pulled him out into the squeaky, sparkling snow.